# AMAZED BY YOU
### RIDING TALL 2

## CHEYENNE MCCRAY

Copyright © 2024 by Cheyenne McCray LLC

All rights reserved.

No part of this book may be reproduced in any form or by any electronic or mechanical means, including information storage and retrieval systems, without written permission from the author, except for the use of brief quotations in a book review.

This is a work of fiction. Names, characters, places, and incidents are either the product of the author's imagination or used fictitiously. Any resemblance to actual business establishments, events, locales, or persons, living or dead, is entirely coincidental.

# CHAPTER 1

"Well, hell." Jayson McBride raised his Stetson, pushed his fingers through his hair, and plopped his hat back onto his head as he stared at the spectacle that had invaded his ranch. "Never making a bet like this again. Might never make another bet of any kind."

Jack flashed a grin and nodded in the direction of the intruders in front of Jayson's barn. "Maybe we'll meet one of those models with their asses damn near showing."

Jayson rested his arms on the top rail of the corral. He glared at his fraternal twin who should have sympathized. "Those ladies are at least fifteen years younger than us. I need that like I need a hole in my head."

Truth was, Jack hadn't dated in a few years, since his wife had passed, and likely wasn't interested in young models. But Jack did like giving Jayson a hard time.

"Options." Jack said before adding, "Monty did say the fashion designer herself is a looker and right in your ballpark."

Just hearing Monty Tinsman's name caused Jayson to scowl again. "He also said the woman is a witch in high heels." Jayson sighed. Another part of this ordeal to deal with. "She's supposed to be here tomorrow." He glanced at Jack. "Why don't you show her around?" He wasn't hopeful, but he gave it a shot.

"Sorry, but I think I'll be busy." Jack didn't look the least bit sorry. "I'm sure you'll handle her just fine."

Jayson glanced down at Thor, who sat on his haunches. "What about you? Maybe you could keep her company."

The Border Collie tilted his head and stared up, his intelligent eyes seeming to say, "Don't look at me, buddy."

Jayson shook his head and stared up at the cloudless Arizona sky. He glanced toward the conglomeration of vans, makeup artists, wardrobe stylists, hairstylists, and set designers. Then there was all the camera equipment the photographer and fashion designer had deemed necessary for the shoot, and who knew what else.

Not to forget a meal wagon—the smells of dried-out pizza and overcooked corn dogs actually overpowered the odor of manure. Yeah, that was some nasty crap in that wagon.

At least nine models were supposed to be in and out of the commercial shoot in less than a week's timeframe. At least that was what Monty said, and Jayson wasn't sure he could trust the man after this. Nine models and four days to a week of shooting, print and film, for a new clothing line.

*Great.*

He hoped his ranch would still be in one piece when they all finally cleared out.

He looked up at the clear sky again and wondered if it would stay that way. In central Arizona, during monsoon season, a storm could sweep in before they knew what was happening. Rain was a blessing for a state experiencing a long drought. This was one time Jayson prayed rain would hold off this week so that this circus would be out of town in a hurry.

"Here comes your favorite person." Amusement rode Jack's words. "He's looking mighty proud of himself."

*Bring in the clowns.*

Monty Tinsman ambled toward them, his belly bouncing as he walked. The muscles in Jayson's shoulders knotted.

Thor let out a low rumble. He hadn't liked Monty from the moment the man stepped onto the Flying F.

Jayson should have listened.

The owner of a decent spread at the foot of the Bradshaw Mountains in Prescott, Monty was a part-time Arizona resident who headed to upstate New York in the summer. Apparently, he'd told the designer of a clothing line he'd do her a favor, and she could use Monty's ranch to do the shoot.

A poker night, a few beers, and a damned glorious bet. Now, the whole mess was in Jayson's front yard.

Monty reached Jayson and Jack, and the bastard grinned. His over-the-top thousand dollar Stetson, two thousand dollar Tony Lama boots, movie star-white teeth, and tanning bed tan didn't make him look any more like a cowboy than Jayson looked like one of those slick movie stars. Monty seemed to be a good guy, though, unless you counted sticking Jayson with this mess.

"I'm surprised you'd show your face around here." Jack grasped Monty's hand. "Good to see you, Mont."

Jayson grumbled under his breath, "It's far too soon."

Monty laughed. "I figured there'd be no problem with the magazine switching locations to your ranch, Jayson." He appraised their surroundings. "I've got a nice piece of property, but yours puts mine to shame."

"I had a full house, ace high." Jayson shook his head. "And you beat me with a royal flush."

"That was some bet." Jack nodded. "Don't feel bad, bro. With your hand, I'd have been all over betting a shoot on the ranch against that prize bull of his."

Monty chuckled.

Jayson wanted a do-over.

But what was done was done. His younger sister Bailey's

voice rang in his mind with one of her favorite sayings, *"Suck it up, Buttercup."*

Where'd she get that crap from anyway?

Jayson shook his head. One of the worst things was a sore loser, and he didn't intend to start down that path. But that didn't mean he couldn't give a little payback if the opportune time arose.

"I've got work to do." Jayson put his hand on Monty's big shoulder. "By the way, I hear paybacks are a bitch."

Jack snorted. "I'd watch your back if I were you, Mont."

Thor gave a throaty growl, as if in agreement.

Monty laughed, then took a look at Jayson's expression. His laugh weakened and faded away. "I know you're not serious—" His throat worked.

Jack chuckled. "I would take Jayson's word on this one." Still grinning, he added, "I best be on my way too. My horses aren't going to ride themselves."

He nodded his goodbye to Monty and flashed a quick grin at Jayson before taking off.

Jayson slapped his hand on Monty's shoulder. "See you around, Mont."

The man nodded. "Sooner or later."

"Unfortunately it's likely sooner." Jayson headed toward the barn with Thor at his heels, and held back a heavy sigh as he worked his way through the crowd.

All this for a damned clothing line?

"No, no, no, *no*," shouted Trevor, the photographer who was no wider than a sheet of paper. As thin as he was, it was a wonder he could hold his monster of a camera.

Trevor braced the camera on his knee and snapped his fingers at the model in front of him.

In the background, several cowhands gawked. Jayson needed to pay them a visit since they seemed to be distracted by a slip of a woman in a skimpy outfit, instead of doing what he paid them to do.

Trevor snapped until he caught the model's attention. "Mina, pay attention. I don't want to see you staring at any cowboy asses. Leave that to me."

The young woman smirked and struck some kind of pose Jayson imagined was supposed to be sexy. The blonde wore skin-tight jeans on her Coke bottle hips and a crazy-ass top that bared her belly. This was what was popular now? Jayson knew nothing about fashion and could care less.

Jayson preferred strong women, and the country girls he knew kicked ass and took names. They did not look like they just walked out of a Scottsdale boutique on their way to a spa treatment.

A lot of the country girls around these parts cleaned up real well and were sexy as hell. All without worrying if they were going to break a nail while rounding up cattle.

That fashion designer hell on heels, who'd be arriving tomorrow, ought to be interesting. No doubt, she'd be one of those women who screamed at the sight of a horsefly and couldn't figure out what to do with a horse if her life depended on it. He wondered what she'd do if she was told she had to shovel shit for a week to do her damned photoshoot here.

*Yeah, that might be fun to see.*

Thor stayed close and they dodged a hairstylist and a man from the food wagon before ducking into the cool recesses of the barn. Jayson blinked a few times as his eyes grew used to the dim light.

He'd owned the Flying F since he was in his late twenties. Back then he and his buddies thought it sounded flat out hilarious to name the ranch "I don't give a Flying Fuck," only shortened to "the Flying F."

Shiloh snorted from one corner of the barn. The pregnant

mare made the sound in a way that told Jayson the horse was concerned about the commotion going on outside.

"It's okay, girl." Jayson reached Shiloh and stroked the brindle mare's nose. "Sorry about that damned mess out there. I'm going fix it, but it looks like I need to talk with the gal running the show tomorrow." He traced the star on her forehead with his fingertips. "But if it's too much for you now, I'll take you over to Justice's place, where it'll just be you and a few of your equine pals."

Shiloh whickered.

"Yes, I mean it." Jayson nodded. "I don't want you upset, girl."

She snorted and bobbed her head.

"Deal." He patted her neck. He normally would have taken her for a ride. But she was so close to foaling, he wouldn't ride her hard like he needed right now.

Jayson moved to Starlight's stall. The chestnut jerked her head up and down. The mare was high strung to begin with, and the noise outside the barn wasn't helping anything.

"Why don't you, Thor, and I escape this madhouse and go for a ride?" Jayson slid his fingers down her neck.

Thor barked.

Starlight snorted and bobbed hear head again in sharp movements. Yeah, she was going to be one hell of a ride today.

"Well, then. Let's do it." He glanced where his cowhands were too busy staring at the model. "But first I need to have a talk with some of my men who aren't doing what they should be."

It wasn't like them, but they had work to do. With the size of his operation, too much needed to be done to stand around doing nothing but looking at a nearly naked woman.

After Jayson gave his men a good talking to, and they were back to work, he returned to the barn.

The Border collie stayed close to Starlight as Jayson grabbed a bridle, a horse blanket and his saddle. When he'd saddled up the mare, he checked her over to make sure she was ready to go in every sense of the word. He grasped her bridle and led her out the rear entrance of the barn, the opposite direction of the insanity that was currently his ranch.

"OH, CRAP." Celine Northland knelt on one knee to gather the many pages from a stack of scattered papers. They'd slid out of the handbag she'd just dropped in the middle of the ramp leading from the airplane to a place she'd rather not be. "Just one more fantastic thing to add to this absolutely perfect day."

*Not.*

Passengers squeezed by to either side of her. Not one person stopped to help her retrieve the sheets of paper.

A child tore by and trampled one of the signature pages of a document she needed to sign and return to Monty, her CFO. The girl left a perfect imprint of a small and very dirty shoe where Celine was supposed to sign.

"Aaaand thank you very much." Heat crept up Celine's neck as she looked over her shoulder. "Where the hell are your parents, anyway?" she muttered under her breath.

A young woman holding a naked doll hurried up the ramp. The woman's hair was slipping from a French braid and red sauce stained her white shirt. She zipped past Celine and trampled another one of Celine's pages. "Chloe!"

*Celine groaned. Question answered.*

*Kids.*

A sheltered only child—of parents who were each only children—Celine had grown up with a series of private tutors and nannies. Celine hadn't often been around kids her age, or kids of any age for that matter. She wouldn't know what to do with one of the little monsters if it landed in her lap.

*God, help me.*

Celine snatched up the soiled papers Monty had scanned and emailed to her, but she hadn't had a chance to read yet. After she had gathered everything into her arms, she shoved the lot into a folder and stuffed it back into her Louis Vuitton tote with her laptop. She hitched it up on her shoulder, her purse on the other, and headed up the gangway.

Bright sunshine poured in through the massive windows. She'd never been to Arizona, but she'd heard the usual about Phoenix—you could fry an egg on the sidewalk or bake brownies on a dashboard. And she'd heard the constant refrain, "But it's a dry heat."

Celine didn't bother peering out the windows for more than a cursory glance. Airports weren't generally known for allowing passengers a view of much more than tarmac and the usual building clutter. Airports were such messy things.

She'd been in countless locations around the globe since she was old enough to travel without a nanny. She'd just about seen it all.

Her parents had never wanted to visit Arizona. Too hot, they'd said. If Celine moved to this state, she likely wouldn't see her parents unless she dropped in on them in their luxury Manhattan condo.

Not seeing her parents. Now there was a benefit to moving to a place like this.

She sighed. What she wouldn't give for parents who actually cared. Her heart ached and she had to push the thoughts and feelings aside.

Celine didn't pay much attention to her surroundings, too focused on making her way to baggage claim. Maybe she'd lived in Manhattan for too long. Like every other New Yorker, she kept her eyes focused ahead and didn't meet a stranger's gaze.

*Like the saying went, Things to do, places to go, people to see.*

A breeze came in from the sliding glass doors as she passed them on the lower level, the wind shifting her long silk skirt around her legs. Her outfit was of her design. She wore low heels for comfort, but frequently wore higher heels. She was five-ten, but with three-inch heels she reached six-one, intimidating for most men below that height. But she wasn't going to stop wearing high heels just to make a man feel good about himself.

When she'd reached baggage claim, she tapped her foot as she waited for her luggage. The way her day had gone, her bags might have ended up in Pittsburgh.

*Stay strong. Have hope.*

*Someday. Someday they'll be here.*

She'd always figured if a person paid for first class then her luggage should be off the plane first. Never seemed to work out that way.

Of course, her two hard shell suitcases came up the conveyor belt last, but at least they'd made it to Phoenix with her. She secured her luggage and headed out to catch a cab.

The airport wasn't exceptionally busy, and within fifteen minutes she was on her way to the AAA Five Diamond Scottsdale Princess Resort in North Scottsdale. One of Celine's select few friends, Meredith, had told her she had to go to the Princess when she came to Scottsdale. Meredith knew fine resort living and knew it well.

The sunshine and the warmth didn't surprise Celine—she'd never been to Arizona, but she'd seen plenty of photographs. What did surprise her was just how much she liked the view. She'd thought the Phoenix desert would be far too barren for her tastes. But what she saw through the cab's windows, between the airport and the Princess, called to her in a way that mystified her.

Clear blue skies and an endless stretch of land that went on for miles, gave her an aching desire to explore this place, so different from any location she'd been before.

Breathing room. She had none of that in New York City. She couldn't begin to imagine what it would be like to live in a place with so much *space*.

And it *was* a dry heat. No humidity to cause her hair to go curly or melt her insanely expensive designer, supposedly unmeltable, makeup.

*Bonus points for Arizona.*

Celine tapped her fingers on her purse. She needed to focus on the commercial shoot and the print ads. She'd been doing her best to not think about what had become a complete headache. She had to go to a ranch tomorrow, for however long it took to get the commercial done. A ranch somewhere in the middle of nowhere.

*And horses. I'll be near horses.*

Her throat ached and she shoved the thought aside.

Why couldn't Rod have found a place in North Scottsdale instead of going for Monty's lame rustic ranch idea? From everything she'd read, Scottsdale was much more civilized than Prescott. But she'd only get to spend the one night here, and then off to the Arizona wilds—or so she imagined.

Celine leaned back in her seat and sighed. To top it off, the location had ended up being selected on a *bet*, and she'd heard the cowboy who owned the ranch was none too happy to have them. Well, she certainly wasn't happy about the situation, either.

She pictured the owner. What was his name? Something like Jack? Jerry? No, it was Jayson. Likely the man was an old, weatherworn cowboy with skin as tough as leather and wrinkles like sand dunes. Probably walked bow-legged on top of that.

At least Trevor, her photographer, loved the ranch. He had visited the original location and said this one was superb—far better with more opportunities for a great photoshoot and commercial.

The models had complained about the smell of cow manure until Trevor had threatened to take shots with the models shoveling shit. Celine smiled to herself. Apparently that had shut them up.

Damn, but she loved Trevor. He was a complete pain in the ass, but he was sharp, knowledgeable, artistic, and just flat out the best in the business. He was worth every damned penny she paid him. And yes, he had assured her, he did shit gold bricks with perfect edges.

She braced her elbow on the cab windowsill, put her head in her hand, and stared out without seeing.

Celine wasn't sure how she was going to do on the ranch. It had been a long time since she'd been close to horses. Her belly took a dive and the wine and cheese she'd had in first class curdled. It would soon come back up.

It had happened so long ago. How could the pain still be so deep? She should be over it now.

She should have forgiven herself, but she never had.

*Do I deserve to be free of that guilt?*

She didn't think she ever could be. Or if she even wanted to be free.


CELINE RECLINED on her hotel bed and idly stared into a glass of Chardonnay that reflected the bedside light. The stack of papers from Monty lay scattered on the comforter beside her. She'd been putting off looking at them.

*No doubt, more money out than in.*

She needed another drink.

Celine idly played with the soft material of her burnt sienna dress. She loved silk, and she loved the soft flowy outfit she had designed. One benefit of her career—she could create whatever she wanted to wear.

Her phone rang and she picked it up from the nightstand. *Monty* lit up the screen.

She sighed. Lately hearing from Monty meant more bad news than good. She wanted to answer with *"What now?"* but settled for, "Hi, Monty."

"Bad news." He sounded dead serious.

Then she did say, "What now?"

"I don't suppose you've listened to the news today?" he said.

She frowned. "No time. Why?"

He sounded genuinely agitated. "Big ransom malware attack all over the damned globe."

Her brow furrowed. "Speak English."

"A hacker syndicate sends out a 'bug' that takes over a company's computer systems and encrypts all their data. They demand money to give you back control of your own computers. That's why they call it ransomware."

Her heart nearly stopped beating. "And you're telling me this because…"

"You got hit with it, Celine," he said. "Twenty thousand."

She almost didn't dare to ask. "Twenty thousand what?"

"Dollars," Monty said. "They've ransomed every bit of computer access to your financial records as well as all of your designs. If we don't pay them, they'll delete everything."

"No." The word came out on a moan. "Don't tell me that."

"I'm sorry, kid."

Celine banged the phone against her forehead. *Not now.*

Her head hurt when she brought the phone back to her ear. "What do you recommend?"

"You don't have a choice," he said. "But I'll make sure you won't ever get hit again. I'll get you the best computer protection money can buy."

"Okay." She sighed. "Do it."

"I'll take care of everything," Monty said.

Celine hung up. The Bearer of Bad News kept giving her more bad news all the time. She should have thought to ask what "the best computer protection money can buy" would cost her.

"This sucks," she said and dropped the phone onto the mattress. Now she couldn't decide if she should review the papers Monty had given her, to get the bad news out of the way all at once—or ignore them in favor of drinking more wine.

The wine won.

She took a long swallow. Screw sipping.

*What about my bank accounts? Business and personal?* She frowned. *Could they have been attacked, too?*

Celine slid her laptop out of the tote beside her on the bed, then booted it up. Maybe she wasn't the most tech savvy person, but she could find her way around a computer pretty well.

First, she checked her personal and business bank accounts. Her business account looked a little low, but then she'd had to spend money for one thing after another—necessary expenses per Monty.

Next, she did a Google search for software that would protect personal computers from outside attack. Multiple links popped up and she chose the most promising. When that company proved useless, she made her way through three more before she found one that could potentially work.

She never mixed her personal accounts with her business accounts. Monty had said he would be happy to take care of both, but she had declined. She needed to have control of *something*.

When she finished, she shoved the laptop into her tote and sagged against the pillows again.

Hopefully she'd protected her personal accounts. But she was out the door already on the twenty thousand ransomed from her business accounts.

*This sucks.*

Her mobile rang again.

"Go away," she wailed.

She glared at the screen, then relaxed when she saw *Meredith*.

"It's so good to hear your voice," she said in way of answering.

"You hadn't even heard it yet."

"I don't care," Celine said. "You could just breathe and I'd be happy."

Meredith laughed. "What's going on? Homesick?"

Celine didn't know what it was like to be homesick. She shook her head. "Long day, that's all."

Meredith knew about Celine's business and about a lot of the people in it, but Celine never shared financial issues. She never talked *business* with friends.

Not that she had many friends. A handful, if that.

"Come home and let Rod, Trevor, and Monty handle this commercial thing." Meredith's voice pressed into Celine's head, forcing her to pay attention.

Celine sipped from the glass. "Liquid courage," some said. Celine simply considered it to be a fluid way to deal with crap or just plain forget.

Meredith's voice tugged Celine to the present. "I saw a gorgeous new pair of earrings at Tiffany's."

"I have to stay." She wanted to cry at the thought of all the money she had to pay out, not counting the ransomware blackmailing thing. Instead, she swallowed the rest of her drink, then raised her empty glass. "Apparently, I need more wine."

Meredith groaned. "Celine, what's going on?"

"I'm okay." Celine had never had a female friend like Meredith. She had made her way into Celine's life until she had to admit that Meredith was a special person, and one of the best things that had happened in her life. "This is my career and I need to take care of business."

Meredith's sigh was audible over the phone. "I suppose you're right. I just worry about you."

"I know." Celine smiled. "You're a wonderful friend and I love you for it." She set her wine glass on the nightstand. "I'm tired and I'm going to get some sleep."

"Sounds like a plan." Meredith yawned. "I didn't realize it's so late. It's nearly midnight here."

Celine laughed. "You knew exactly what time it is. You just wanted to check on me."

"Busted." Meredith's grin was clear in her voice. "Good night, Celine. I'll talk with you tomorrow. Got it?"

"Yes, ma'am." Celine's smile lasted until she said, "Good night," and disconnected the call.

She looked at the wall across the bed while she sipped wine. She really didn't know if she'd be able to sleep.

Maybe she needed to start going to a shrink. Mother had always thought therapists and psychiatrists, and the best possible meds, were the answer to everything. Mother would have been livid if she had known Celine spit out the meds they had forced her to take for so-called depression.

Celine had not been depressed. She'd been hurt, sad, in pain, and heartbroken…but mostly filled with devastating guilt. That didn't mean she needed drugs. Some people did, and that was okay. But she hadn't.

However, her mother had seen to it the psychiatrist prescribed some designer antidepressant that had cost a ridiculous amount every month.

And her mother's voice—it rang in her head, as if she was in the room, with her correcting, criticizing, ordering, demanding.

*Take your medicine, Celine. It's for your own good.*

*Be calm and act like a lady.*

*Ladies do not cry.*

*Do what you're told or you will regret crossing me.*

*Don't wear that. You look fat in it.*

*A kindergartner could put on makeup better than that.*

Celine gritted her teeth and closed her eyes. *Stop it. Stop the mom-voice before it really gets up to speed.* Her arm ached to throw her glass in the cold fireplace.

She took a deep, calming breath and let herself relax. She imagined tension leaving every part of her body.

In spite of brick walls she'd had to break through, she had started her own business from scratch and broke into a tough industry during a financial downturn. The success of her business had been amazing.

Now she needed to take amazing and boost it into incredible. She needed everyone's eyes on her designs. With a successful launch of her latest line, her designs would be in stores across the country.

She smiled. She'd worked her butt off to get here without using the checking account Mother and Father had set up for her when she was young. She had taken what money she had used for college and repaid every cent back into that account, including interest.

It had been so important to pay her way, create, and become successful on her own.

And that was exactly what she'd done.

Celine set the wine glass on the nightstand and sank into her pillows. Part of her need for success was to be able to donate to a cause that meant more to her than anything. A charity that brought Arabian horses and underprivileged teenagers together.

She didn't know a lot about kids, but she did remember what it was like to be a teenager, and how healing a relationship with a horse could be.

Her heart constricted as she thought about Sky. What an amazing horse she'd been. Her best friend, her confidant. And then she was gone…and it had been Celine's fault.

In the future, she wanted to own a ranch that used horses for therapy with teens. She wanted kids to experience what she had when Sky was alive. And she wanted them to learn from her mistake.

Celine didn't drift off for a long time. Eventually she slipped into a fitful sleep. She dreamt of Sky galloping in an open field, before darkness fell. In the black of night, the only thing she saw was the word *Merf,* scratched into a wall.

## CHAPTER 2

Bright June sunlight nearly blinded Celine and she blinked, attempting to accustom herself to it and the heat as she climbed from the dim interior of the black Mercedes. She managed to get out with her Louis Vuitton handbag on one shoulder. In her opposite hand, she gripped the matching tote that held her laptop, along with the stack of papers from Monty.

She congratulated herself for staying on her feet after the harrowing ride. She shot a look at Charlie as he got out of the driver's seat. He'd nearly killed them sixteen different times in sixteen different ways.

"I'm going to murder Monty," she muttered under her breath. Bringing Charlie to something so important, something that would be launching her new line—Monty should be shot.

"Miss Celine." Charlie jogged around the front of the car. "What time do you want me to take you to the hotel in Prescott?"

*Never.*

"I've already made arrangements." She told him the lie while she held out her hand. "Keys."

Charlie looked disappointed and handed the set to her.

She gestured toward the set. "I'm sure they can use you someplace over there. Ask Rod."

*Go brighten someone else's day.*

Now Charlie was Rod's problem. Considering Rod was the one who sent Charlie to get her at the hotel in Scottsdale, fair was fair. She'd kill Monty and set Charlie on Rod—there, two vultures taken out with one stone.

How Charlie had gotten her to the Flying F Ranch alive, she had no idea. He was a walking disaster, not to mention a driving nightmare. She was amazed he was able to pilot his drone without crashing into something.

Celine glanced up at the clear blue sky then squinted as she looked at the chaos of the shoot, which should have been more organized. The day was already growing hot, but from what she understood, it was quite a bit cooler in Prescott Valley than the Phoenix metropolitan area.

She took a moment to scan the country around her. Monty was right. The ranch and the surroundings were spectacular. She'd been told the ranch was at the base of the Bradshaw Mountains and the country was even prettier than what she'd seen on the ride from the airport to North Scottsdale. She had to agree.

The mountains surged upward, behind the ranch. It was an awe-inspiring mountain range that looked as if the Almighty had placed it in the desert. She'd have to get someone to show her the entire property.

It was all far too much to process without some coffee. Good coffee. She'd forgotten to take the premium Panama blend with her to the hotel, where they'd had a mediocre ground brand.

Lucky for her, she had an entire bag of the whole bean stashed in Monty's trailer. With her name on it.

"Thank the heavens." A woman on a mission, she strode straight to the silver Airstream trailer Monty had insisted on but rarely used. Charlie, his nephew, used it more than he did.

She avoided eye contact with anyone—she didn't want to risk

being waylaid. As a New Yorker, it was second nature to ignore everything but her destination. She knocked on the Airstream's door, gave it two seconds, and jerked the door open. She tossed her handbag and tote onto a couch. The tote looked like it would slide off, but she glared at it and the thing stayed put.

*Yes, I am officially a witch.*

It took her all of thirty seconds to discover her coffee wasn't where she left it. The bag should have been in a far corner of the pantry, where she always kept extra for emergencies.

She began to plot murder.

Her plans grew more defined the longer she looked for it.

The door slammed open. She turned to face it and saw Charlie duck his head in.

*If he had anything to do with it being gone—*

Charlie got one look at her face and took a step back. "Didn't mean to bother you, Miss Celine. I'll just—"

"Stop." She held her hand up. "Do you know what happened to the Hacienda la Esmerelda coffee I had in here?" She pointed to the exact location. "The bag with *my* name on it?"

Charlie's throat worked. "The guys ran out of coffee. I didn't think you'd—"

She was certain a blood vessel would pop in her head.

"Charlie." She spoke in a slow, measured tone. "You had better get back to work right now."

She'd never seen him move so fast. He didn't even stop to close the door behind him.

Celine turned and put her fingertips to her forehead. *Just coffee. Just coffee,* she tried to tell herself.

*Just one of the finest coffees in the world. Lifesaving coffee to everyone here.*

A knock at door frame of the open trailer door. *Charlie?*

Celine turned and came to a hard stop. Words stuck in her throat.

One of the sexiest men she had seen in her life—and she'd

seen a lot in her career—stood in the doorway. His eyes were shadowed by a western hat, but his firm lips and lightly stubbled jaw hinted at the man beneath. A T-shirt stretched from one amazing pectoral to the other, hugged shoulders to die for, and clung to tight abs and straight down to hips made to straddle. And those Wrangler jeans cowboys tended to wear out here in the Wild West.

*Oh. My. God.*

"What can I do for you?" Her voice came out harsher than it should have.

The man pushed up the brim of his hat with one finger and she got a good look at his ice blue eyes. She'd seen eyes like that on a male model once, and she'd thought she'd never seen a more beautiful man. She wouldn't call this man beautiful. She'd call him a chili-hot cowboy stud.

She almost put her hand to her heart that thudded too hard and way too fast.

He didn't show any emotion as he appraised her. And that was exactly what he was doing—appraising her. "Did I catch you at a bad time, Ms. Northland?" His smooth voice would have stolen her breath if she hadn't already lost it.

No doubt, a cowboy here to find out what she needed for the shoot.

She straightened her stance. "Rod is handling anything to do with the set. I'm sure he can help you." *Although I wish I could.*

"He sent me to see you." The man stepped into the trailer without invitation. "I understand you run the show."

Wow, wasn't often a man towered over her. With her height, she wasn't used to being around a man she had to look up to just to meet his eyes. With her two-inch heeled sandals, today she was six feet and he topped her by at least four inches.

Now, here was a man to snuggle up to.

She had to work to keep her composure. "Depends on what you need, Mr.?"

"Jayson McBride." He took off his hat and held out his hand, even as he continued to eye her steadily. "Call me Jayson."

*So much for wizened old tough-as-nails cowboys.*

Celine knew she should soften her stance and her tone, but she felt caught off guard, as if in a compromising situation.

She took his hand and shivered inwardly as a bolt of *something* shot through her. What the hell was that all about?

"How can I help you, Jayson?" She drew her hand from his. She'd intended to lighten her tone, but it came out as hard as concrete.

"You could help me a lot by packing up and leaving." His tone was even, yet had an edge to it. "But since that is likely out of the question, I'd like you to choose a different part of the ranch."

"The contract you signed gives us free rein. My staff determined this as the best place to start the shoot." She shrugged. "We've got a lot invested in this." She moved past him and out the door. "We'll only be a week," she said as she headed down the trailer steps, and came to a full stop.

A chestnut mare stood nearby, fully saddled, complete with a shotgun in a leather scabbard hanging on the side of the saddle. The mare had a spirited look in her intelligent gaze.

Celine hurried to turn around so that she wouldn't have to look at the horse. Jayson had followed. A Border Collie now stood at his side, head cocked, looking at her with warm, intelligent eyes.

"Frankly, I don't want you here at all," Jayson said and her gaze shot to his. "The least your people can do is respect my property."

Her jaw tightened. "If it wasn't for your gambling habit, we wouldn't be here."

A shiver rolled through her as Jayson's eyes turned hard and storm-dark. "I play poker with friends," he said in a cutting tone. "Doesn't mean I have a gambling problem. What I do have a problem with is how your people have taken over and how they're doing it."

She pushed her long hair over her shoulder and placed her hands on her hips.

He continued, "They're in the way and have made everything a mess. They've toppled a corral, moved things around that I want to stay put, and are generally getting into things they shouldn't be. They leave gates open. Only stupid people leave gates open on a ranch."

A shadow passed over them and they looked up. Charlie's drone circled the trailers. Charlie leaned up against the rail of a corral as he used a controller to dictate the drone's movements.

She looked back at Jayson. His features had tightened even more. "That drone spooked my cattle and they trampled a fence. My men and I had to round them up and repair the fence line."

He narrowed his eyes. "Get that drone down," he said. "Or next time I see it I'll shoot it down and have the taxidermist mount it and put it on the wall next to Big Jimmy."

Heat prickled her skin. "You hunt?"

"I aim to start if I see that drone again." He set his jaw. "The damn thing spooked my cattle and upset my horses. I won't put up with that. I have a mare ready to foal who's getting real nervous."

The moment he'd said "horses," her skin chilled and she went still.

"I'll fix that for you." Celine broke through the icy shell that had temporarily immobilized her. She moved to the mare and rested her palm on the shotgun's stock. "May I?"

Jayson appeared to be taken aback. "All right."

"Loaded?" she asked.

"Uh-huh," he said slowly.

A quick few seconds and she held the shotgun, barrel pointed up. "Are your horses used to guns, especially her?" She nodded in the direction of the chestnut.

"They're all gun-trained," he said in his low cowboy drawl. "Including Starlight."

"Good." Celine turned and looked in the direction of the drone. She raised the recoil pad to her shoulder and sighted the drone. She waited until the thing was clear of humans and animals alike, then squeezed the trigger.

*Boom.*

The shot echoed throughout the foothills .

The drone exploded. What was left plummeted and slammed into the dirt.

Everything and everyone fell silent. She'd had it with Charlie and that damned thing.

"That was a $5,000 drone," Charlie wailed and started to come closer.

She narrowed her gaze.

Charlie stepped back.

Celine turned to Jayson. "What else can I do for you?"

He watched her as if for sudden movement. "You can get them to leave my things alone and to close the damn gates."

She turned to the staff that gaped at her. "Next one to leave a gate open, or get into Mr. McBride's belongings without permission, will get an ass full of buckshot. You'll be picking it out for the next week." She glared at all of them. "Have I made myself clear?"

Rapid nods from everyone.

"Then get back to work." Celine turned back to Jayson. "Can you get a list to me of approved locations my people can use?"

*His eyes seemed to say, Who are you and what have you done with the woman I just met?* "I'll do that."

"Thank you." She rubbed her temples again, pressing against them with her thumb and forefinger. She handed the shotgun to him. "I'm sorry. I've had a rough couple of days." She shook her head. "And I am coffee deprived. It's dangerous to be around me until I have a few cups."

A moment of additional appraising, then the corner of Jayson's mouth quirked as he took the shotgun. "I've been known to cut off a few heads before a pot of good ol' cowboy coffee."

"Let's start over." She held out her hand. "Celine Northland. I'm the fashion designer for Celine Originals, and you know the rest."

He shifted the shotgun to his left. "I'm Jayson McBride. I own this hunk of Arizona." He took her hand and a charge went through her that caused her to catch her breath. "I'm certain I don't know the rest. But after that shooting demonstration, I'm sure there's a lot more to the story."

It took a moment for his remark to sink in. "It's nothing special." She smiled. "I imagine you have a few stories to tell." She tried to withdraw her hand, but he held it just a little bit longer.

"Why don't you come on in for cinnamon rolls and coffee?" He nodded in the direction of the place she'd barely acknowledged when she arrived. "That is, if you can handle sludge that'll grow hair on your chest."

She breathed a sigh of relief when he finally released her hand. "Sludge?"

He flashed her a grin that would make a lesser woman's knees weaken. "Just sayin' I put more than twice the amount in the coffee pot than is called for. My sister, Bailey, says you can stand a spoon in it."

Celine grimaced. "Sounds...like it would probably get me through this before anyone gets decapitated." She glanced at the people scurrying around them. "No, decapitation is still a possibility."

Jayson grinned and shook his head as he slid the shotgun back into its scabbard. "Come on over."

She pushed her hair over her shoulder. "Give me about fifteen minutes to take care of a couple of things and get my Xena sword."

Jayson took the horse's reins and gave Celine a questioning look.

She shook her head. "Never mind. I have to get coffee before my Hyde side returns."

He gestured in front of them. "Ladies first."

She walked past. "I always heard cowboys are notorious for being gentlemanly."

"Notorious, huh?" He and the Border Collie fell into step with her as he led the chestnut mare. "Is that a good thing or a bad thing?"

"Right now, it's a good thing." She glanced at him and found it refreshing to not be eye-to-eye to a man or looking down. She'd always liked a tall man, and Jayson qualified.

Not to mention he qualified for a whole lot more.

She almost groaned aloud. She'd better stop thinking this way or she'd need to have her head checked when she got back to New York.

Rod stood on the path in front of them as they walked around the trailer.

"She let you live?" Rod said to Jayson. "When Charlie told me about the coffee, I thought you were a goner for sure. And then when she got out that shotgun…"

"You're half the reason I need so much coffee." Celine narrowed her gaze at Rod. "Send Charlie to pick me up again, and they'll be scraping you up off the ground."

Rod made a poor attempt at looking concerned. "I'll keep that in mind."

"You'd better." She turned to Jayson. "You've met Rod."

"Yep." Jayson gave a nod.

Celine said, "I'll take care of the issue we spoke about and a couple of other things, and then meet you at the house."

"I need to turn out Starlight, but that won't take long," Jayson said. "When you get to the house, come in through the back door. Everyone does, considering that's where the coffee is."

"Believe me, I'll be there in no time."

"I'll have a mug waiting." He turned and headed toward the barn, leading his mare beside him, the Border Collie at his heels.

Celine pivoted and glared at Rod. "We have to get the operation away from Mr. McBride's horses. Do it now."

---

AFTER TAKING off her saddle and blanket, Jayson had turned Starlight loose in the corral since he intended to ride her later. He strode from the barn to his home.

He held back a grin and glanced down at Thor. "I've always had a weakness for strong women," he said to the dog.

Celine Northland qualified. He didn't think she was a witch, like Monty had said, but he could be wrong. He wouldn't tolerate anyone who was abusive, whether man or woman.

When he'd knocked on the doorframe and she'd spun to face him, he thought her glare would singe his body. He could almost smell the scent of burnt hair.

He'd also thought he'd been in for a battle to get rid of that damned drone and get their operation away from his horses.

But the moment he'd said "horses," she had turned on a dime. He wondered where she'd gotten that concern from.

*And holy shit.* He hadn't known what to think when she'd asked to use his shotgun. But when she'd shot that drone out of the sky he'd been afraid he'd bust a gut laughing at the looks on her employees' faces. It'd been all he could do to keep a straight face.

He stood back as Thor trotted in. Jayson let the screen bang shut behind him and left the kitchen door open. He hung his Stetson on the hat tree and breathed in the scents of coffee and cinnamon rolls. Couldn't get much better than that.

When he was in the mood for cowboy coffee, he kept the coffee warm on the burner, which gave it an even stronger flavor. The cook had left a pan of homemade cinnamon rolls on the counter, covered in foil. His cousin's wife, Tess, had hired a fantastic cook for Jayson and his staff. Tess knew food and the way to a dozen men's stomachs, and she'd used her expertise to get him a great cook. Almost as good as Tess, which was saying a lot.

After he made sure Thor had water and dog food, Jayson looked in a cabinet and grabbed two of his biggest mugs and two plates. He loaded each plate with an Arizona-sized cinnamon roll and filled each mug with coffee. He had no doubt Celine would be in the kitchen before her coffee could cool.

The moment he set the mugs on the table, Celine opened the screen door and entered the kitchen. Thor sat on his haunches and watched her come in.

"Phew." Celine wiped her forehead with the back of her hand. "I am not used to this heat."

"Welcome to Arizona." Jayson studied the dark-haired woman. "If a newcomer makes it through his or her first summer, then they stand a good chance of coming back."

"Right now, the only thing I care about are those smells." She closed her eyes and breathed deeply. Her stomach growled loud enough for him to hear. "Coffee and cinnamon rolls," Celine said. "I have died and gone to heaven."

Jayson grinned. "Have a seat."

She opened her eyes. Before she could move to the table, Thor plopped his butt right in front of her path. She paused and looked down at him. Thor thumped his tail on the tile.

Jayson watched Thor, wondering what the dog was up to. He'd never behaved this way, and he'd never been overly friendly with anyone.

Celine hesitated. "Hi, boy." She glanced at Jayson. "May I pet him?"

He nodded.

She crouched to Thor's level. The dog ducked his head, allowing her to touch him. She slid her fingers through the

Border Collie's silky black and white hair. "You're so soft." She didn't look up as she stroked him. "What's his name?"

Thor never invited anyone to pet him. Jayson wondered if the dog was getting soft. "Thor."

"What a nice boy." She scratched behind his ears. "And friendly."

"Not usually." Jayson had a hard time reconciling the normally cautious dog with the one now becoming buddy-buddy with the fashion designer. "Coffee is getting cold."

She stood then moved to the table in the alcove. She slipped onto a bench in front of a full mug and a filled plate.

Jayson grabbed paper napkins and joined her, mentally shaking his head at the dog now settled at Celine's feet. What did the dog know that he didn't?

Celine took a long drink of coffee and choked. "Jeez. You weren't kidding this *is* strong. I can already feel hair growing on my chest." She shook her head. "Thanks for the warning."

"My pleasure." He watched her take sip after sip of the coffee.

Celine was beautiful as hell with long almost black hair and eyes a dark seashell-brown. It was an unusual color, but on her it was fantastic.

He drank from his own mug, mostly in gulps as opposed to sips. He got up and grabbed the pot and set it on a trivet at the center of the table, along with the pan of cinnamon rolls. One wasn't going to be enough, despite their size.

"Bless you." She sighed and pushed her mug forward. "I feel Mrs. Hyde going back into that little box inside. As long as I get my coffee, no one will get hurt."

"Noted." He poured another cup of his sister Bailey's idea of sludge. "I will keep it in mind in the future."

She smiled and it was like the sun breaking through clouds and shining on him.

"Now that I'm coffee-fied, I'm ready for a sugar rush." She pulled off a sticky piece of her roll. "I haven't had homemade cinnamon rolls since Cook Nancy." Celine's features seemed to relax more.

"Cook Nancy?" he asked.

She nodded. "One of many cooks who passed through my parents' kitchen. She was my favorite and lasted the longest. She somehow managed to put up with Mother *and* Father." Celine sighed. "But everyone has a breaking point."

He ate another bite of cinnamon roll then licked frosting from his fingers. "You like horses," he stated.

Celine went very still, like when he'd first mentioned his. A light rose tinged her cheeks.

She picked at her cinnamon roll and didn't look at him. "Who doesn't?"

Something was there. An old pain, an old regret. Now was not the time to push the topic. One day he would learn exactly why she reacted the way she did when he mentioned horses. He would pick at the ice she'd coated herself with until he broke through.

He mentally shook his head. Why would he think she'd be around long enough for him to get that far?

"So, what's this all about?" he asked. "Why are you here? Not because I lost a damned bet. What are you doing, and why do you need a ranch to begin with?"

Celine's shoulders visibly relaxed. "As you know, I'm a fashion designer." She waved her hand in the direction of the chaos outside. "We're going all out with my new line. It's pretty much do or die."

Jayson nodded, letting her fill the gaps with her story.

"The last two lines were considered successful," she said, but it clearly wasn't enough. "They paid the bills and the reviews were fine, but not raving."

She leaned forward, her cinnamon roll forgotten. "I need raving. I need phenomenal."

"You think this will do it?" he asked.

"I feel good about it." Celine's expression grew more intent. "We used crowd funding to get people involved, so they would be invested in the line. The plan is to use that funding and support to blast out of the gates."

She looked even more intense as she went on. "I have the financial backing from an investor, in addition to the crowd funding. We are going to tear the fashion world apart and insert ourselves big time."

He nodded, enjoying the passion and fire in her eyes.

"Once we're all wrapped up here," she said, "we'll be pushing our campaign in print, on TV, and using social media. YouTube, Facebook, Twitter, Instagram, blogs—you name it, we'll do it."

"Admirable," Jayson said and meant it. "I try to stay away from social media, but I have an employee who makes sure to keep us visible. I hear it's a good way to get the word out."

"Yes." She laughed. "If we could, we'd even get into the video game market. Can you imagine a fashion game?"

He grinned. "Not even close."

Her gaze drifted away, like she was seeing inside herself instead of the room she was physically in.

She returned her attention to Jayson. "We're going to make this happen, and Celine Originals is going to be big."

"I believe you." He found himself caught up in her dream and her enthusiasm. "I have a feeling you can do anything you set your sights on."

Celine smiled. "We use cutting edge digital tech and fantastic handcrafted traditional textiles. This line is going to blow everyone out of the water."

"I'd like to see what you're doing on my land." He looked at her intently. "I'm interested in your venture."

She studied him and nodded. "Sure, I'll show you anything you're interested in. But first you and Thor need to take me on a tour of your property."

"Done," he said. "When's good for you?"

She looked out the kitchen window, sighed, and shook her head. "I need to find out what the hell is going on out there and make sure everything is under control."

"Why don't you have dinner here, and bring some photos and show me your designs?" He drew her attention back to him. "Tonight, if you don't have anything going on."

"No plans." She smiled. "I'd enjoy having dinner with you. Will Monty join us?"

Jayson scowled. "He's lucky to be alive. It'd be safer for him if he stayed away."

"Make that double." Celine grinned "I was ready to do him in after I made it through the ride with Charlie." She went on, "I have an iPad and all of my designs are on it. I'll bring that to dinner with me."

"Sounds great," Jason said. "Need any more coffee?"

Celine paused and tilted her coffee mug to peer inside. "Empty, but my indicator is on full again." She glanced at her plate that had only a few crumbs left before meeting Jayson's gaze again. "The rolls were amazing. Thank you for both."

Jayson gathered the plates and mug as he stood. "Let me know when you're ready to take that tour."

"I'll find you this afternoon and we can plan it."

Thor came up beside Jayson and they watched her rise and leave the kitchen. Damn but she had a fantastic backside. Not to mention front side.

Jayson put the dishes in the sink before he grabbed his Stetson off the hat tree and headed out to get some work done, Thor at his heels. There was always something to do on the ranch.

# CHAPTER 3

The moment Celine came out the kitchen door, she knew her hair was going to go curly.

She looked up at the sky and her eyes widened. Clouds rolled in at a fast pace. Dark clouds heavy with rain.

"Are you kidding me?" She pushed her formerly smooth hair away from her face. "It was clear and bone dry when I got here, and now it's going to storm?" She ground her teeth. "Just what we need."

The screen banged shut behind her as Jayson followed her outside. She cast a look over her shoulder. She wanted to kick her own ass for the instant attraction she felt toward Jayson. Her whole body sang with need. She hadn't felt real desire for any man for longer than she cared to admit. But now, with Jayson…

It wasn't just desire for this man. Something else was there that made her question her sanity.

"Storms come up quick around here this time of year." Jayson swept his gaze over the horizon as he and Thor came to a stop beside her. "Living in the mountain's shadow has some benefit, such as a decent amount of rainfall during our monsoon season, compared to lower parts of the valley."

Celine looked at him incredulously. "You're great with this?"

He gave a slow nod. "We're in the high desert and we've been having a drought for more than a decade. We need every drop we can get."

"I'm surprised you wouldn't be upset." She glared at the sky. "If we get rained out, we'll be here that much longer." She couldn't afford to pay the team for days lost, not with how money had been flying out the window for one expense after another.

Jayson hooked his thumbs in his pockets. "That's true, but like I said, we need that water." He went on, "Often we get short spurts, and that's frequently in small pockets across the valley rather than one big storm that covers the entire area."

"And that's important how?" she said.

"Seems like you didn't have enough coffee." Was that amusement in his eyes?

She narrowed her gaze. He'd better stay on her good side—she still had her Warrior Princess sword, and she knew how to use it.

Before she could share that fact, he said. "You might send some of your crew to do an indoor shoot for today. We've got a nice mall about ten miles from here."

"Ten miles?" She looked at him in surprise. "That's your closest?"

"Yep." He nodded. "Or you could hang out here and hope it lets up." He pulled his phone out of his pocket and opened a weather app. "Today's forecast calls for a good deal of lightning and thunder, part of a strong storm developing in this part of the valley."

She shook her head. "This sucks with a capital S." Okay, so *sucks* wasn't so mature, but she wasn't feeling real adult right now. "I don't *want* to adult today," she muttered as she looked up at the sky. "You can't make me adult."

A brilliant burst of lightning cracked the sky.

The heavens opened as if the lightning had torn open a rift in the dark, swirling clouds.

Huge drops of rain fell, as thunder rumbled loud enough to shake the ground.

Celine sputtered and wiped mascara from her eyes with her fingertips. "Now what?"

"Get inside," Jayson said behind her. "There's lightning in the distance, and you never know if it'll start here."

Lightning flashed, illuminating the dark sky for one moment. Celine groaned.

"Plenty of towels, so you can dry off in my house," he said. "You can wait out the storm."

"I need to talk to Rod and my photographer." She had to shout over another roll of thunder. She hoped James had managed to get his equipment out of the rain.

Jayson said. "Got a few things I need to take care of, too."

She was pleased to see the trailers had been moved farther away from the barn, per her instruction before she went in for coffee with Jayson.

"Does this happen all the time?" Water plastered her face as they walked away from the house.

Water rolled off the brim of his western hat. "During monsoon season, we like to hope it will."

She scowled at him. "Night would be a more considerate time to rain."

"I've never heard of the desert being considerate." He grinned and started toward the barn. "I'm going to check on the horses."

An ache developed in her head. She hated how the backs of her eyes prickled every time horses were mentioned. *Damnit.* She had put that world behind her so long ago.

How could she still hurt so deeply after all these years had passed?

*A voice rang in her mind. Your fault. It was all your fault.*

How could she have known?

That didn't matter. It was ultimately her fault. The storm muffled her words. "I should be over it by now." But she wasn't.

*Stop it, Celine.*

She stepped into a puddle and her sandal slipped in mud. She yelped as both feet slid from beneath her.

Mud splattered her face and covered her clothing as she landed on her butt hard, jarring her teeth. She just sat in the puddle liked a piglet in a bathtub filled with mud. Of course the piglet would have been ecstatic.

Celine held up her arms, trying to process that she was covered nearly head to toe. The ick she'd landed in smelled as if she'd fallen into a wet pile of manure.

She looked up at the sky and rain washed her mud-spattered face.

Today she hadn't worn her own fashion design. She'd decided to wear more conservative clothing. She groaned as she looked down and assessed the damage. Prada sandals, annihilated. Dior slacks, ruined. Vera Wang blouse, destroyed. Victoria's Secret bra and panties, history.

"A fine mess you've got us in, Celine." Mess was right.

Should she scream? Cry? Laugh?

A giggle escaped her before she could stop it. She clapped both hands over her mouth and accidentally smeared her face and lips with more mud.

She sputtered and spat the ick. "That's so gross."

Yet another giggle rose and this time she let loose with laughter. It continued to rain, but she sat in the smelly pile of mud and crap and laughed.

"Are you all right, Celine?"

She looked up to meet Jayson's face as he crouched beside her. He might have been concerned, but his eyes were filled with laughter.

"Go ahead." She grasped a ball of mud from the bottom of the puddle and raised it. "Laugh and you'll be wearing this.

On your face." She narrowed her gaze. "I'm a pretty good shot."

"You don't have to worry about me, honey." Jayson's eyes still glittered with restrained laughter. "I've seen you shoot a drone from the sky. I don't need any other proof."

*Honey?*

"I'll sure as hell laugh." Monty chuckled as he came closer. "I doubt you could hit the broad side of a barn if you were five feet away."

"Really." She snapped her wrist and flung the mud ball at Monty.

It splattered across his face.

Thor barked, as if in approval.

"Right on your barn-sized nose," she said while laughing at the astonished look on Monty's face. "You very much deserved that."

His tone grew harsh, angry. "You—"

Celine nailed him again.

Cheers and laughter filled the air and Celine glanced up to see some of their staff gathered round.

She looked at each man there—almost the whole team was present. Of course, the women members of the team were too smart to be standing around, laughing at the woman who signed their paychecks.

"Anyone else want to try me?" Celine asked.

"I wouldn't." Jayson's voice came out in a rumble. "She's got an arm like a pro."

Celine rolled her eyes. "You heard the man."

Snickers and more laughter.

All out of giggles, Celine decided she was ready to get out of the puddle now. She was becoming wetter, stickier, and stinkier by the moment.

"Come on." Jayson held out his hand.

She took it, and he pulled her to her feet with the strength she had sensed before.

"Thank you," she said when she was steady.

"I've got a mudroom." He inclined his head toward the house. "Let's get you in there and cleaned up."

"Yes, let's." She ignored the remnants of laughter, but continued to enjoy Monty's sputtering. She didn't feel the least bit sorry for him. After all, he was the one who kept giving her bad news

*So, I shot the messenger.*

She giggled again.

They walked toward the house, Thor trotting at her side instead of Jayson's. The rain had stopped.

"Didn't it just get started?" Celine eyed the sky suspiciously. "It dumped on me, gave me a nice puddle to take a mud bath in, and it's already over?" Clouds drifted apart, allowing the sunshine through. *"Really?"*

"Yep." Jayson nodded. "That's an Arizona monsoon for you."

She could imagine how she must look as he opened a door and gestured to it. "You'll feel a lot better with that mud off."

"And smell a lot better." She gave a self-deprecating grin. "Not my finest moment."

"You can laugh at yourself," he said. "I like that."

"It's either laugh or cry, and I choose the former," she said. "I prefer to avoid pity parties altogether. That doesn't mean I don't have I-can't-believe-this-crap-happened-to-me moments, or I'm-going-to-kill-you-if-I-don't-get-coffee days."

Jayson chuckled and shook his head.

Thor stayed outside as Jayson followed Celine into a room with a shower at one end that had frosted glass for privacy. Two industrial washing machines took up space on her right, with a large sink on the left, next to a double-sized fridge and a deep freezer.

She gestured to the freezer. "For the bodies of unsuspecting people who invade your property?"

"Nah." He shook his head. "Those we bury on the back-forty. But don't worry. The graves are well hidden."

Celine reached the middle of the room, standing on tile the same color as the mud now drying on her clothing and body. She faced Jayson. "I have really got to get out of these clothes. I feel like I fell into one of those cow pies you have in the corral."

"No comment," he said with a wink as he walked past her and locked the door leading into the house. "When you're finished, you can wrap up in one of these towels." He opened a cabinet filled with dark brown towels, across from the shower, and pulled one down for her. "Then come on into the house."

"I don't suppose you have something more than a towel for me to wear until I can get other clothes?" she asked. "Maybe a T-shirt?"

He hung the towel on a hook beside the shower. "My kid sister is about your size and leaves a change of clothes or two for the times she's home from college and stays at the ranch."

"Thank you." Celine's shoulders relaxed as she started to unbutton her blouse. "I haven't checked into the Prescott hotel yet, so my bags are in the car." She cocked her head to the side. "I left my purse in Monty's trailer, and my keys are in it."

"If the sun is still shining, we can get your bags once you're clean and feeling human again." Jayson glanced through a window. "It's clearing up, at least for the time being."

"Sounds like a plan," she said.

He touched his finger to the brim of his hat. He left by way of the back door into the house. She locked it behind him, just to make sure none of his ranch hands walked in on her. She wasn't worried about Jayson. The man was polite and considerate from what she'd seen.

At this point, Celine wouldn't have cared if Jayson *had* stayed. All she wanted was the shower. She turned it on and let it run until it was warm while she stripped out of what were now nothing more than filthy rags. There was no bringing silk and other fine materials back from the dead.

So, Dior, Vera, and Victoria went straight into a garbage bin next to the towel-stocked cabinet.

What had she been thinking when she dressed this morning? She hadn't.

Back when—she swallowed—even then she'd known better than to wear nice clothes anywhere near a place that needed a barn. Guess she'd just been away from that world for too long to have any common sense left.

Yeah, common sense would have been a big help all right.

The Prada sandals she rinsed off in the shower before setting them on the floor outside the stall. They were ruined, too, but she could at least wear them until she got to the Prescott hotel. Tomorrow she'd head to the mall and find herself some sturdier shoes than what she had with her. She had plenty of undergarments in one of the suitcases in the car, but she needed jeans and T-shirts for the ranch.

When she stepped under the warm water, she melted into the spray. "This feels wonderful." She took the washcloth, poured on the unscented soap, and scoured her body. She made sure she was entirely mud-free and stink-free by staying under the spray and cleaning up for a good fifteen minutes. The warm water was heaven after that mud bath.

She grabbed the huge man-sized towel that she could have wrapped around herself twice. She let her wet hair fall around her shoulders and grabbed her sandals before entering the house. The air-conditioned air chilled her refreshed skin, but in a good way.

"Feel better?"

Jayson's deep voice startled her into grabbing her shoes tight to her chest as she whirled to face him.

She relaxed. "You do know that scaring me has consequences."

He grinned. "Honey, I have a feeling just being around you has consequences."

If any other man had called her honey, he might have found himself on his ass. She might not know martial arts, and might not have any fighting skills, but she did have her Xena sword somewhere... Well, so it was a plastic sword Meredith gave her as a joke for Christmas, but no one needed to know that.

She had a feeling that knocking Jayson on his butt would be tough, but she'd enjoy every moment of trying.

Her face warmed. If he only knew the direction of her thoughts...

"You can change in the guest room." He held out a bundle of clothing. "These are some of Bailey's, work clothes. She keeps her horse here while she's in college, and takes care of him when she visits."

Celine took the stack and her body became instantly aware of him with the slightest brush of their hands. Her nipples tightened beneath the towel, and a thrill went straight from her belly to between her thighs.

Her throat worked as they stood and stared at each other for a long moment. His eyes seemed to burn, the heat reaching out to her and drawing her in at the same time. Did he feel the same connection?

She did her best to regain her composure and took the stack. His fingers slid over hers again, scorching her, and for a moment she didn't think she'd be able to breathe, much less think.

"The guestroom is down this hall." He turned and a wave of relief washed over her. She'd go crazy if these feelings didn't stop. Being near him for much longer was dangerous to her mental health.

Somehow, she kept her voice steady as she tried to match his pace. "Is the sky clear?"

"For the time being." He slowed so that she could keep up with him. "It's raining something fierce higher in the mountains, and a storm is rolling in from the south. Probably a good idea for your people to head into Prescott and come back in the morning."

"That sucks." She blew out her breath. "What's a few thousand dollars down the drain? When I've already lost so much?" She muttered the last part to herself.

"As a businessman, I can understand the value of time and money." Jayson glanced at her. "But this time of year, we have to be careful. Flashfloods frequently come down the arroyo from the mountains and they can be deadly."

"Sounds serious." She hugged the clean clothes to her chest as they walked. "Do you think it will rain in the morning?"

"It's hard to tell this time of the year." He shrugged. "You're fairly safe in the mornings, but the storms are unpredictable. They tend to build up early to late afternoon."

"Good to know." Her mind ran through potential plans. "That means we need to get our work done in the mornings, as early as possible. Morning light is just going to have to do it."

"No guarantees one way or another, but that's probably a good idea." They stopped in front of a doorway. "Here's the guestroom. When you're dressed, head down that hall." He pointed in the opposite direction from the way they'd come. "You'll know where you are once you hit the kitchen."

"Great." She tried to smile as she stepped into the room, but what she wanted to do was draw him inside with her and take full advantage of the perfect male specimen he was.

*Guess my body is more alive than I thought.*

In truth, it had nothing to do with being more alive, and had everything to do with Jayson McBride.

"I'll be there in a few." She smiled brightly, while wondering what it would be like to see him with his clothes off. *Down, girl. Down!* "It won't take me long at all."

The corner of Jayson's mouth quirked, as if he'd heard her thoughts. "Coffee?"

She gave an enthusiastic nod. "A quick cup would help clear the fog."

Jayson left and closed the door behind him. Celine slid on Bailey's Wranglers that were so worn they were soft. They fit Celine a little snugly across her hips and her thighs, but otherwise perfect. The pink T-shirt stretched tight across Celine's breasts, but felt comfortable.

After she slipped on the sad-looking sandals she'd rinsed off, she carried the towel with her as she walked in the direction Jayson had pointed.

When she reached the end of the hall, she took a slight jog to the left and walked into the kitchen.

Jayson was in front of the open fridge, his back to her. She studied his backside, enjoying the play of muscles beneath his T-shirt as he looked for something. Who knew what, but she hoped he'd do it longer so that she could stare at her leisure.

She sighed. It must have been loud enough to hear because he looked over his shoulder and gave her a sexy grin.

Heat prickled her scalp. *Damn. Busted.*

He turned and let his gaze drift over her from head to toe, like she'd just done to him. "Those clothes fit you just fine."

She nodded. "Thank Bailey for the loan, please."

Jayson nodded as she pushed hair over her shoulder.

Damn, it had really curled now. She sighed and tugged on a curl. "No straightening iron handy, I imagine," she said, with no hope whatsoever.

He cocked his head. "A what?"

She pulled out one of her curls. "I go curly when it's humid or rains. I prefer it straight, not that it matters right now."

"I like it that way." He gestured to the curl she was playing with. "You look cute with curly hair."

She raised an eyebrow. "Cute?" No one called her cute. She didn't remember ever being called cute, except maybe as a child.

"Yep." He nodded. "Ready for that coffee?"

She let the curl pop back into the rest of the mess. "Yes, please."

He reached for a mug out of the cabinet, filled it from the pot on the stove, then handed it to her.

*Their fingers touched again. Damnit. He's doing that on purpose.*

She put the mug to her lips then made a face as she drank the coffee. She emptied the mug and handed it back to him. "My chest is going to be extra fuzzy after that cup."

He laughed. "Would you like more?"

She shook her head. "I need to get my team out of here for the night. We can come back in the morning."

He set the mug into the sink. "You won't be here for dinnertime since you'll be heading back to Prescott with everyone else, so how about lunch tomorrow?"

She smiled. "Deal."

Jayson walked outside with Celine. Thor barked from across the barnyard and bounded toward them. He immediately went to Celine and she rubbed him behind his ears as she looked up.

The sun shone through sparse clouds, and it smelled wonderfully of rain. "It's beautiful out here. It's clearing up."

"Don't let that fool you." He frowned as he looked to the north, where dark clouds clustered. The sky had turned dark gray beneath the clouds. "Looks like it's raining like the devil in the mountains. Probably a good idea for you all to get going so you don't get caught in a flood or stuck here for the night."

She nodded. "I'll get everyone out of here."

They walked closer to the trailers and she did the one thing she knew would get instant attention. After a good ear-splitting whistle that made birds scatter from the trees, she had everyone's attention in a moment. "If it floods, all of us may have to stay overnight in the trailers or the barn instead of in Prescott. So get in gear and let's move it. That is unless you would prefer the barn over the hotel."

When Celine's crew was motivated, they could haul ass. She'd never seen them get everything together so fast since she'd started working with them.

She didn't drive much in New York City because she walked or took cabs everywhere. However, this time she insisted on driving herself to the hotel in Prescott. She wasn't about to let Charlie drive her again, she was irritated with both Rod and Monty, and she didn't want to spend time in a car with idle chitchat that she might have to participate in with anyone else.

It wasn't that she was antisocial—well, not really—it was more she wasn't in the mood to talk.

In truth, she wanted to be alone in her own thoughts, and just maybe let them settle on Jayson McBride.

She groaned to herself. *Pull it together, girl.*

Celine hurried to Monty's trailer to get her purse and tote from where she'd left them on the couch. The purse was there. The tote was not.

She hurriedly searched for the tote, but couldn't find it anywhere.

Someone honked outside. Damn it. She'd have to look tomorrow. She left the trailer and headed across the muddy ground for the rented Mercedes.

Ahead, a line of vehicles was already leaving the ranch.

According to Jayson, his men had left a good thirty minutes ago, after making sure everything was set to the foreman's approval. Jayson sent them off so they could spend time with their families as opposed to getting stuck here for the night.

Jayson perched on Starlight. He and Thor watched as the convoy took off. Celine gave Jayson a brief wave before she slid into the buttery soft leather covering the driver's seat.

She fished the keys out of her handbag, then tossed the purse onto the seat before she secured her seatbelt and started the vehicle.

Celine followed the small convoy away from the ranch. As they drove, she glanced up through the sunroof. The sky was dark again from the incoming storm. Any time now and it could let loose another torrent.

She peered ahead as they reached the edge of the property and she saw the dry arroyo Jayson mentioned. It was as wide as a small river. Funny, she hadn't even noticed it when Charlie drove her here. Maybe it was because she'd been grateful just to be alive at that point. Jayson had made it clear to everyone to not enter the wash if water was present.

Nope, they were fine.

Her phone rang as she drove behind the other vehicles. She paused just long enough pull her phone from her purse and glance at the caller ID. *Meredith.* She answered and brought it to her ear.

"Hi, Meredith," Celine said as she gripped the steering wheel with one hand. "How did your day go?"

*Mine turned out surprisingly well.* Despite the mud bath and harrowing ride this morning, she felt pretty great.

Meredith gave an exaggerated sigh. "It was hell. Just hell."

Celine stepped on the gas and entered the arroyo. She'd fallen behind the others. "Tell me what happened."

She glanced to her right as she reached the middle of the bed of the arroyo.

Fear ripped through her like a blade.

A wall of churning brown water rushed straight toward her.

## CHAPTER 4

Celine screamed.

Fear barreled through her like the wall of brown water bearing down.

The phone flew from her grasp as she grabbed the steering wheel with both hands.

She punched the gas. Her sandal slipped off the pedal.

The wall of muddy water slammed into the Mercedes.

Terror expanded in her chest in a cold ball that grew ever larger as the water lifted the car at least five feet off the bed of the arroyo.

She caught sight of the bumper of Rod's car a moment before the car twisted and she screamed again.

On the opposite side, she saw a flash of Starlight tearing down the road with Jayson, heading straight for the raging flashflood.

Meredith's frantic shouts came through the receiver of the phone sliding around on the floor as Celine was jostled.

The vehicle bounced against rocks and boulders lining the arroyo. Metal creaked. Water sloshed across closed windows and sprayed into the car. The river-sized flashflood roared around her.

Celine felt as if her heart would explode. The car flipped again and raced backward with the flood.

Water started to fill the Mercedes, the flow growing faster and faster as the vehicle sank. The flood had to be at least five feet high.

The vehicle slammed into an embankment and came to a jarring stop.

Celine's pulse raced, adrenaline pouring through her.

She had to get out of the car.

Had to get out before she drowned.

She unfastened her seatbelt and pressed the button to lower the window. It buzzed two-thirds of the way down and stopped.

She looked up at the sunroof. She found the button and managed to get it a few inches before the car moved and her fingers slipped.

She was flung against the partially opened driver's side window.

Water the color of chocolate milk sloshed over the lowered window and slapped Celine's face. The fluid went up her nose and she coughed and sputtered as dirt and debris filled her mouth.

She pressed the button repeatedly to lower the window, but it wouldn't budge.

More floodwater rushed into the car.

*She had to get out. I have to get out. Now!*

Could she squeeze through the window opening? She could be trapped if she got stuck.

She'd be trapped if she didn't.

The car sank faster and faster. She didn't have time to think about it. She had to *try*.

She turned back to the window and pushed her upper body through the opening.

Water roared past and covered most of her. If—no when—she got out, she might be swept along with the power of the flood.

The water slapped her brutally as she wriggled through the partially opened space.

Debris hit her shoulder and a branch punched her back, nearly knocking the breath from her at the same time pain lanced her body.

She squirmed harder. Her hips stuck in the opening. She tilted her head back to keep the rising, thundering water from covering her face.

Celine pushed and wriggled and got her hips through. She freed herself and surged to the top of the water outside the car. She frantically grabbed for something to hold onto then grasped the partially lowered window. Then her fingers slid from the glass.

She screamed then grabbed the mirror before she could be swept along with the flood. Her hands slipped.

Something caught her ankle and jerked her below, submerging her completely.

Muddy water obliterated her vision as it covered her. She would see nothing even if she tried to open her eyes.

What held her ankle? A root. Had to be.

A log rammed the back of her head. Stars sparked in her mind. She struggled to maintain consciousness. She couldn't pass out or she'd be swept away.

Celine fought the feeling and forced herself to ignore the pain. She grasped the driver's side mirror again and struggled against the root holding her under.

Her lungs burned. How much longer could she hold her breath? Panic nearly overrode her.

She fought to have some semblance of calm as she tugged and yanked and twisted.

The root gave way.

Celine shot up. She lost her hold on the mirror and immediately slammed against a long tree branch. She broke the surface and sucked a deep breath into her burning lungs. She grabbed onto the branch before the floodwater swept her down the bank.

Rain came down in a torrent.

Lightning flashed. Thunder boomed.

A branch scraped her temple.

The car shifted and started to move.

Celine screamed, terror overriding every other thought.

*Get on top of the car.*

She held the branch with one arm, shoved herself up, and managed to get her knees on the Mercedes' lowered window. The narrow glass bruised the skin below her knees.

The car shifted against the bank again. It started to move.

She grasped the crevice of the partially opened sunroof.

With all her might, she dragged herself onto the top of the Mercedes. She'd lost her sandals and crouched barefoot on the metal, precariously close to the small opening of the sunroof.

Celine had only a moment to catch her breath before the car jerked away from the bank.

She lost her hold on the branch.

Her fingers slipped as she tried to cling to the frame of the partially opened sunroof window. She held on as tightly as possible. What if she lost her grip? Water rushed around her and the car. She'd be dragged under and carried away with the floodwater. She'd never make it.

*No.*

Celine gripped the opening tighter with both hands and pulled herself to her knees. She didn't let go, wouldn't let go.

The car banged against the opposite bank before bouncing off a tree and spinning backward.

Rain poured down. The lightning seemed brighter. Thunder louder.

Her fingers slipped on the window opening and she clenched tighter.

Celine searched the bank as the car bounced against it. Could she grasp a branch or bush and hold onto it?

She had to try something. The car was still sinking at the same time it was being shoved along in the flood barreling through the arroyo. Only a portion of the roof was above the water.

"Celine!"

A male voice barely carried over the rush and roar of the flash flood. A dog barked repeatedly.

Celine jerked her head around, frantically trying to find who had yelled at her while praying that person could help her.

*Jayson.*

He rode Starlight along the bank, keeping up with the car. Thor was on the bank, barking, encouraging her to hang on.

The Mercedes came to a hard stop.

Celine slipped and screamed as she slid off the roof.

She gripped the window opening.

Debris pelted her body.

Another crack of thunder.

Her muscles ached and burned. She didn't know how much longer—

No. She had to fight as long as it took. And Jayson was here.

But her body was so tired.

*Tired, so tired.*

"Celine," he shouted again.

She looked up to see she and the car were now facing the bank and Jayson.

He held a rope and shouted. "Grab the rope!"

She barely had the strength to hold on and raise one hand. The car was almost under water.

He whirled the rope into a lasso over his head. He released the rope.

The lasso settled over her head and dropped over her shoulders

Celine shifted so the rope slid to her waist.

"Hold on," Jayson shouted as the rope tightened around her.

She grasped the rope with both hands.

He pulled, dragging her off the roof.

Fear slammed into her as the last bit of sanctuary vanished below the surface of the water.

She clung to the rope as Jayson dragged her through the raging water, closer to the shore. Starlight walked backward, helping Jayson bring her in. Thor clamped the rope in his jaws as he helped pull.

More debris. More foliage. Scratching her, hitting her, covering her.

Closer to the bank. Closer.

The rope caught on a branch.

Celine struggled to pull the rope off the branch but her energy was rapidly fading and the rope wouldn't come free.

Thor bounded into the water and swam toward her. He grasped the rope and tugged until it finally came free.

Jayson reeled her in, closer to shore. "Come on, honey," he said. "I've got you."

Thor released the rope and swam beside her. She flung her arm over his neck as he and Jayson worked to get her to shore.

A few feet more and they reached the bank.

Celine collapsed onto the earth. She'd used every bit of her strength. Her muscles would no longer work.

Jayson dismounted the same time she reached shore. He pulled her the rest of the way up and brought her into his arms.

She struggled, feeling as if the current was dragging her down again. The flashflood continued to roar as she coughed and spit out muddy water.

"I've got you." Jayson's voice soothed her as he wrapped her in his embrace. "I've got you, Celine. You're all right."

Lightning seared the sky. Thunder rolled.

She stared up at Jayson, barely able to comprehend or understand. She blinked then slipped away.

ADRENALINE PUMPED through Jayson's body as he gathered Celine tighter. She looked so damned pale and cuts bled on her arms.

A hard thump in his chest caused a powerful ache as he stood. He had to get her home, assess her and treat her. No way could he get across the arroyo now. The massive strength of the flood had disintegrated the road from his ranch to the outside world. What was left was a mini-canyon, and the flood continuing to rage.

Jayson held Celine tightly as he dodged debris that had been flung onto the bank from the churning water.

On the opposite side of the raging flood, he heard shouts from Celine's people.

The ground shook as lighting flashed a network of bolts across the sky and thunder boomed. Rain fell even harder, partially obscuring Jayson's vision.

Celine shifted and her eyes went wide as she regained consciousness. She started fighting to free herself. *"No."* She coughed and struggled. *"Help."*

"Relax, honey." Jayson's heart hadn't stopped thundering, even as he held Celine's wet, shuddering body. "I've got you. You're going to be okay."

She went limp again, but when he looked at her, she was still conscious.

He glanced at the flashflood. A rattlesnake was swept along with the current like a stick. "We'll get you warmed up," he told Celine.

Her teeth chattered and body trembled, as if her body would never stop reacting to the trauma. He gripped her tighter, wanting to share his body warmth with her, even as rain continued to pour from the skies.

The wind snapped a branch from a tree and it landed in Jayson's path. He nearly stumbled over it, but made it over the thick branch. He wanted to stop and check her for any serious injuries, but he had to get her warm and to the house.

He hurried to Starlight. When he reached the horse, he looked at Celine. "Can you ride?"

That strange stillness, then a nod.

"I'm going to put you in the saddle," he said. "Hold onto the pommel. I'll ride behind and make sure you don't fall."

She nodded again. "Okay." The word sounded raspy.

He helped her up, and she slid into the saddle as if she'd done it many times before. She gripped the pommel as he unstrapped the blanket behind his saddle and wrapped it around Celine's shoulders.

Jayson swung up and settled himself behind Starlight's saddle. He grasped Celine around her waist with one arm and the reins in his left hand. He tugged on the reins slightly to calm Starlight who danced sideways from the extra weight.

He glanced across the water to the opposite bank and looked at the now silent crowd on the opposite side.

"Is she going to be all right?" Rod called out. The unearthly roar of the flood had lessened enough that Jayson could hear the man. "We can take her to the hospital."

Jayson shook his head and pointed to the location Celine's men had crossed. "The flood is too deep, and it also wiped out the crossing. Even when the flood dies down, you don't want to attempt it."

He went on, "She's slipping into shock. I'm taking her back to the ranch and I'll get her warm."

"What should we do?" Rod shouted. "I can call the sheriff's department."

"Do it," Jayson said. "Call me in twenty and we'll trade updates. You have my number."

He made a clicking sound to Starlight. "Come on, girl." He

guided the mare away from the bank and they headed back to the ranch house at a gallop. Thor ran alongside, barking, like he was encouraging Celine, telling her she'd be all right.

The ranch house wasn't far from the crossing. When they reached the front yard, Jayson dismounted, looped the mare's reins around a hitch and helped Celine down from the saddle. He swept her into his arms. Her entire body shook as he carried her to the house.

"Meredith," Celine coughed then spoke again. "We were on the phone. Need to let her know I'm okay."

"We'll tell her." Jayson hoped Rod would know how to get a hold of this Meredith Celine was talking about.

Jayson went in through the kitchen and slammed the door shut with his boot before he rushed through the house. Thor barked while he trotted beside Jayson as he took Celine straight to the master bedroom. Everything he'd need was in the adjoining bathroom.

Celine's shivers had intensified. He took her into his bedroom, then bee-lined it to the bathroom and set her on the closed toilet seat.

Thor sat on the rug just inside the bathroom, concern filling his intelligent eyes.

He turned on the shower, bringing it to a slightly warm temperature before stripping her of her clothing. He cursed beneath his breath when he took inventory of her injuries. Scratches and bleeding cuts covered her, along with red marks starting to purple.

Thunder crashed and Celine's body went rigid. Stark fear crossed her face.

"You're okay, honey." Jayson toed off his boots but left the rest of his clothing.

Her teeth chattered. "It sounds so close."

"We're safe in the house." He scooped her up and took her into the shower, then set her on the smooth tiled ledge on one side of the enclosure. The water wasn't too warm so that he could bring her temperature to normal slowly.

Water rained down on her as he searched her body for injuries. He examined her head as he spoke in a low, calming tone. It was nothing more than mindless chatter similar to what he used to calm an injured animal, or a foaling mare. The idea was to soothe her while he warmed her.

He talked about the Diamondbacks baseball game scheduled to play that afternoon in Phoenix—where they probably weren't getting any rain—and their odds for winning. He told her about the branding in May for the February calves, then went on to tell her about the last roundup.

As he examined her head, she flinched when he skimmed his fingers across the back of her skull as he touched a good-sized egg.

"Ow." It was a low groan. "That hurt."

"Sorry, honey." He asked her questions and she responded to everything in a normal but tired manner.

Slowly, her shivering lessened as her body returned to the right temperature. He relaxed and helped her to her feet but still held her. A feeling of relief flowed over him like the warm spray they now stood under.

He washed her hair with his shampoo. No doubt she'd want the dirt from the flashflood out of her hair, and this would help warm her from the scalp down. He took care not to graze the bruise on her forehead, near her hairline or touch the egg on the back of her skull.

The need to protect Celine and take care of her grew stronger inside him. He barely knew this woman, but it didn't feel that way. He *knew* her. When he saw her being swept away with the flood, he'd felt as if some part of him had been ripped from his chest.

Somehow, on a soul-deep level, he had an incredibly strong connection with Celine.

Jayson wasn't sure whether or not to question his sanity. He had never been one to believe in that kind of thing, but hell, who knew? If he thought about it, he and Jack had one of those twin-connection things that did exist. So, could it be the same with Celine?

That didn't make sense. Did it?

When Celine was clean and warm, he turned off the shower and set her on her feet on a soft rug. He grabbed a thick towel and dried her off, working on every limb. His own rain and shower-soaked clothing chilled him, but he ignored it and focused on Celine.

Until this moment, he had kept his attention clinical from the second he'd stripped her of her clothing. It was hard to remain that way when it was clear she was no longer in shock and she was warm again.

Celine was such a damned beautiful woman, with soft curves and hair that he wanted to nuzzle as he breathed her in.

Jayson ground his teeth, forcing himself to not think of her that way.

"How do you feel?" He sounded much gruffer than he'd intended.

"Better." She went on, "Thank you more than I can say." Her teeth didn't chatter anymore.

He shifted and got a better look at her when she was no longer in his shadow. He saw more of the red and purple marks that marred her skin in multiple places. He frowned. She would sport a lot of bruises, and she'd be sore as hell.

But she was alive.

"You look worse than a bull rider whose been stomped on a time or two," he said. "But I'd sure as hell rather ride a bull than go through what you just did."

She looked at him and her gaze met his. "I sort of feel like I got trampled."

While he studied her, he checked her pupils, and was glad to see they weren't dilated.

Celine winced as he patted a cut on her arm with a soft cloth. "This one's about the worst of the scratches and cuts," he said. "They're mostly superficial, but they sure looked bad when we dragged you out. The bruising and the knot at the back of your head and the one on your temple are likely worse than the scratches. You've got one hell of a bruise on your back, too."

"I can sure feel it," she said. "But considering the alternative, I'm fine."

He grabbed a robe from a hook on the back of the bathroom door. It had been a gift he'd never used, and it was perfect to bundle up Celine to make sure she stayed warm. He helped her into the robe and tied it.

"Thor and Starlight helped you." Celine coughed. "They were amazing."

"They were." He glanced at Thor, who watched them. Jayson turned his attention back to Celine. "Can you walk to the bed?"

"Yes." Exhaustion laced the word.

Jayson met Celine's gaze again, this time taking in her beauty. Damn, those brown eyes captured him and he couldn't look away.

He forced himself to move. He guided her toward the California king-sized bed, but let her walk on her own to make sure she was steady. He pulled the coverings back and helped her slip beneath them.

"Bed." She sounded sleepy and just as exhausted as she spoke. "Never felt this good before."

Her eyelids lowered like weights dragged them down as he tucked the blanket under her chin. For a moment, she looked like she was going to say something else, but she fell asleep almost immediately.

Jayson watched her breathe in and out, the sound restful. It used to be considered imperative that a patient with a head injury stay awake. More recent research showed that wasn't the case. As long as the person who's injured can hold a conversation when awake, didn't have issues walking, and her pupils weren't dilated, it was fine to let her sleep.

He studied her for a long moment. Bruised and battered, she was still a lovely woman. She might have a materialistic, bitchy outer shell—according to some—but she was hiding behind that shell. And he intended to drag her out one way or another.

Jayson didn't want to leave her alone, but he had to take care of the animals and contact Rod, Monty, and the sheriff about her. Best thing he could do right now was let Celine rest and check on her frequently.

He left Thor behind. "Watch over her," he told the dog. "Come get me if she needs me."

Jayson grabbed clean clothing for himself and left the room, leaving the door open wide enough for Thor to get out if he needed to.

His cellphone rang as he headed in the direction of the kitchen. It wasn't a number he recognized, but it was a New York area code. No doubt one of Celine's people.

"This is Rod. Is Celine okay?" The man spoke in a rush. It was clear he was genuinely concerned for her. "Is she going to make it?"

"She's fine." Jayson strode down the hallway. "She's resting now. I imagine she'll need a whole lot of sleep to recover from what she went through."

Rod let out a breath of relief. "I contacted the sheriff's office. He's waiting on your call to see if you need medevac. Sheriff McBride said a helicopter could land in one of your pastures."

"I don't think we'll need emergency services," Jayson said. "But I will keep an eye on her."

"Is there anything I can do?" Rod asked.

"Celine said she needed to let a woman named Meredith know she's okay." Jayson reached the kitchen as he spoke. "She said something about being on the phone with her before she got caught up in the flood."

"She already tracked me down," Rod said. "I told her all I know and that I planned to call her back with more information. I'll do that now."

When Jayson disconnected with Rod, He set his clean clothes in the mudroom. He'd take a shower there after he finished up with the chores.

He headed back into the kitchen to make some coffee as he contacted the sheriff's department where his cousin, Mike McBride worked. Mike had recently been reelected sheriff after a few tough battles, both personal and professional.

"Hi, Mike," Jayson said when the sheriff answered. "You've heard about Celine Northland being caught in a flashflood?"

"Yes," Mike said. "Do you need medevac?"

"No." Jayson blew out his breath. "If she takes a turn for the worst, I'll dial 911."

"Hopefully that won't be a problem," Mike said.

Jayson went on to give a quick rundown on what had been going on with the commercial shoot on the ranch. He explained in full what had just happened with the flood, and that Celine wasn't at fault. She'd been careful, but that hadn't been enough.

When he finished filing the report over the phone with Mike, Jayson asked, "When is Anna due?"

"Not for another three weeks." Mike sounded like a proud dad already. "Anna says she's about to burst."

"Girl or boy?"

"Girl." Mike had a grin in his voice. "Already polishing up my shotgun."

Jayson smiled. "She'll have plenty of cousins who'll keep the boys in line, too."

"Don't you know it," Mike said. "What is going on with you and your clan?"

"Like any other part of the McBride family, as normal as can be expected."

After his conversation with Mike, Jayson called Monty.

"I heard about what happened with Celine." Monty sounded worried as hell. "How is she? Do you need my help? I can take the trail."

"Celine's fine," Jayson told the man. "No need to come to the ranch.

"Thank goodness she's okay." Relief poured over the phone line from Monty. "Can't imagine what she went through."

"It was damned bad," Jayson said. "We came close to losing her to the flood a few times. She's a brave woman and a fighter."

"She sure is," Monty said.

Jayson disconnected. His men had left long ago, heading to their homes and their families. It was better they hadn't been trapped on this side of the arroyo.

He took Starlight back to the barn, brushed her down, and praised her for helping save Celine. He put her in the stall with a ration of sweet oats before checking on the other horses.

The entire time he did the chores, his thoughts kept turning back to Celine. Damn but he hoped she'd be all right.

After having served in the military and the training he'd been through, he had a good feeling that Celine would be okay, but he didn't plan to count on it. He'd keep a close eye on her.

He made short work of the rest of the chores before heading to the house to clean up and get back to Celine. He'd have felt concern for anyone under his care, but somehow it was different with her. He wasn't sure he understood the feelings, but he didn't plan on analyzing them, not right now.

Maybe later. All he knew was that one way or another, he intended to find out exactly what kind of hold she had on him and what he was going to do about it.

## CHAPTER 5

"Thank God the bitch is alive." He wasn't ready for her to be dead. *Yet.* MERF wasn't ready.

Monty tossed his cell phone onto the writing desk. It clunked and spun, coming close to the edge but stopping a hair's width from falling off. He was tempted to flick it with his finger and send it spinning off the desk.

He'd seen the whole thing play out before him from the ridge near his property. When he had watched Celine cling to the top of that Mercedes, he'd alternated between hoping the flood would win to praying she'd be rescued.

Then *he* could kill her when he had everything he needed. When Monty's Early Retirement Fund was nice and well padded, enough to keep him comfortable for the rest of his life in Belize. He'd found a perfect location, and he was ready to put a bid on it.

He hated her and her fucking family. She'd never known who had destroyed what had been so important to her.

With narrowed eyes, he picked up Celine's designer tote that was stuffed with papers and her laptop. Of course, only the best for her, so she'd paid a good chunk of money for the Louis Vuitton bag.

The bitch didn't know what it was like to work in the trenches and scrabble her way to the top.

Celine might not take any of Mummy and Daddy's money now, but that didn't matter. She'd insisted on returning the money for her education to her parents when she made enough from her business to do so.

But he was certain her parents' connections had opened doors. The kind of doors that *he'd* had to pry open with a crowbar. Others he'd never be able to even see through.

As far as he was concerned, Celine didn't deserve a penny of the money coming in.

Soon it would be his.

He took the papers he'd given her out of her tote and flipped through the pages. He came to the signature page and let out a burst of obscenities. *Not signed.* Just a child-sized footprint there and a partial imprint of an adult sized sneaker on the next.

Monty tossed the stack of papers aside. He'd make sure those were signed even if it meant putting a gun to her head.

Next her laptop.

He withdrew it from the bag, set it on the writing desk, and raised the lid. The laptop woke from sleep mode and a retro screensaver with flying toasters popped up with her name and a place to put in a password.

Seriously? She had the old flying toasters screen saver?

With a snarl, he typed in *password*. He couldn't believe people used that as a login.

No such luck with Celine's laptop. He checked his notepad that had a page he'd prepared with dates significant to her—names, places, people, and that one beast, her dead horse.

He tried them all.

*Nothing.*

One more try—

It locked him out.

*Too many attempts. Try again later.*

His muscles ached as he had to restrain himself from throwing the laptop across the room.

*No.* It wouldn't do a damn bit of good if he broke the thing. The last bit of information he needed to destroy her, and to take every penny from her, was on this expensive hunk of crap.

He'd have to try later.

A crack of lightning illuminated the sky outside the window, followed by thunder not three seconds later. Coming closer. One hell of a storm carried on outside as it was.

It reminded him of Celine on her ass in the mud puddle and how she had thrown mud into his face. *Bitch.* He'd wanted to choke her then and there.

The laptop was low on juice, but thankfully, she had put the power cord in the tote. He plugged it in and started charging the battery.

Monty flung himself in the closest chair and chewed on his thumbnail. He'd done that since he was a child and waited for a bottle. Or sat in the corner when he was punished. He'd never been able to stop that damned habit.

*Get back on track.*

This would all come together. He'd worked too hard for it to fail.

He stared out the open window, remembering that night so many years ago when he'd nearly destroyed a little girl's hopes and dreams. Her parents hadn't known what to do with the miserable sniveling brat. That had been one hell of a treat for him to see.

*A disgruntled employee.* He had nearly laughed his ass off when that theory came out in the local paper. The Northlands still had disgruntled employees coming out their asses.

He was far more than a disgruntled employee. This was all about *revenge.*

And it would be sweeter than anyone could possibly imagine.

## CHAPTER 6

*Water swirled around her, catching her up and dragging her away. A bolt of lightning ripped apart the sky. Thunder crashed, the sound reverberating straight through her.*

*Faster and faster she sped down the arroyo. The flood roared in her ears. Water rose higher and higher. Massive waves crashed against the shore.*

*Rain whipped her face and wind chilled her through.*

*The current carried her farther and faster than before. In the distance, she caught sight of a giant whirlpool, like water circling a drain. Debris spun downward and vanished.*

*The flood swept her faster, straight for the funnel disappearing into the bottom of the water.*

CELINE WOKE IN A RUSH, as if shot down a tunnel of light. She gasped and opened her eyes.

Sunlight from a nearby window was too bright and her eyes ached. She grasped the covers and pulled them over her head.

The white sheets and comforter muted the light. She let herself breathe slowly as she tried to piece things together.

The sheets and comforter smelled good—and they smelled familiar. Like a man. Not just any man...

*Jayson?*

She lowered the covers and blinked against the bright light then scooted up in bed. Her entire body ached, as if she'd been pummeled in a boxing ring. Maybe worse. She felt like a limp noodle that needed more sleep as she rested her back against the pillows while she took in her surroundings.

A masculine room, filled with chunky rustic oak furniture. The cushions and coverings were in rust, gold, and brown color combinations.

Definitely a man's room. A couple of cowboy pen and ink drawings mixed with three oils; a few pictures of what she assumed were family members and maybe close friends; and an open closet filled with western shirts and several pairs of boots on the floor.

*Jayson McBride's room.*

Thoughts, feelings, and images rushed back to her, mixed with her dream. She had to sort through them to determine what was real.

What she came up with were horrifying *memories*.

The wall of water slamming into her car. The brutality of being thrown around, battered, and nearly drowned in floodwater. The terror she'd felt had been unlike anything she'd experienced in her life.

She shook her head then regretted it when a sharp pain shot through her skull. Something hard had struck her when she was in the water, like a log.

And then Jayson had saved her. She'd been weakening, afraid she wouldn't make it. Then he was there, throwing her a lifeline.

She needed to find Jayson. She climbed out of the bed, her body protesting with every movement she made. One sharp pain dug into her skull via the back of her head. A second felt like someone had jabbed a knitting needle into her forehead.

"Tylenol," she muttered as she got to her feet. "Anything."

She wore a large men's robe and realized she was naked beneath it. She wasn't sure how that had happened, but considering she'd been in filthy water in a flashflood, she was happy to be clean and in whatever he had available.

A movement startled her. She glanced to the right and saw Thor looking at her. How had she missed him?

"Hi, boy." She held out her hand.

He wagged his tail and went to her, and let her rub him behind the ears.

"You helped save me." She got down on her knees, wrapped her arms around his neck, and hugged him. "Thank you."

Celine drew away and Thor licked her cheek. She smiled.

With Thor at her heels, she left the room and wandered down the same hallway she'd been in before. The smell of coffee hit her full in the face.

*Coffee. Lifeblood.*

The stuff that kept others alive. Around her.

She padded along cool tile as she followed the smell and remembered the way to the kitchen.

She reached the doorway and saw Jayson with his hip against a counter as he looked at a paper in one hand and held a steaming mug in his other. And next to him—

"Is that a Keurig?" Her eyes widened as she walked into the room. "You gave me stuff that'll make my voice turn baritone, and you have a Keurig?"

He looked up from the paper, amusement in his eyes. "Would you like a cup?"

"God, yes." She moved closer as he pulled a rack of coffee pods out of the pantry. "Sumatra or French Roast if you have it. Black."

"Right here." He pulled out a pod and proceeded to make her a mug of Heaven.

While she waited, she scratched Thor behind his ears. When

the coffee was ready, she took it from Jayson and breathed deeply before taking a sip.

"Thank you." She sagged against the countertop. "The world thanks you."

Jayson grinned.

After a few more sips she eyed him. "If you have a coffee maker with gourmet brands, why in the world did you give me cowboy coffee?"

He snorted. "Wasn't too sure if I liked you yet."

She stared at him for a moment, then laughed. "Can't say I blame you." She put her hand to her head. "Ouch. Laughter isn't always the best medicine."

Jayson quieted and let his gaze drift over her. Not in a sexual way, but in an assessing manner. "How do you feel?"

Celine finished taking a sip and raised her head. "Alive. Thank you." She held the mug in both hands. "And that has nothing to do with the coffee."

"You're welcome." He brushed his thumb over her forehead, surprisingly feather-soft. "Damn, woman. You've got bruises everywhere. You're going to be as sore as a bull rider after a hard ride."

"It's true, I'm sore." She smiled. "I'll take your word on the bull rider part."

"It's one thing you don't want to try just to see how it feels." He shook his head. "Cousin of mine, Creed, is a world champion bull rider. I used to compete with him on the local level. Good times."

Jayson shook his head and laughed as he went on. "I guess if you can call three cracked ribs, a shattered wrist, a couple of broken bones, and being gored by a bull good times."

Celine tipped her head to the side and studied him. "I'd say in your case, yes, those were good times."

"And you'd be right." Jayson made himself another mug of

coffee. "Then I headed off to the service for a few years and Creed pursued his passion."

Jayson shook his head. "Now he's settled down. Wife is Danica—sweetest gal from the southeastern part of the state. They have kids and I've never seen Creed so happy." Jayson grinned. "Would never have thought he'd stop the circuit and take on the role of daddy and husband. Guess you had to have known him back then."

"We all change." Celine set her empty mug on the countertop. She had no idea where the contents went. "Tell me about the service."

"First, do you want breakfast?" he asked.

She shrugged. "Maybe something light. My stomach is a little off kilter."

"Oatmeal?" he asked. "Butter and brown sugar?"

"I haven't had that in years." She nodded. "Sounds perfect." She gestured to the coffee maker. "Along with another one of those."

He moved to the open door of a large pantry. "Help yourself while I make breakfast."

She picked out a pod of Sumatra and had another steaming mug in her hands in no time. She found napkins and spoons, along with a jar of brown sugar, a container of real butter, and a package of walnuts.

Jayson served the oatmeal and they doctored it up. Celine wasn't sure when she'd had a better-tasting breakfast. Could be it was so wonderful, because she was alive to eat it? If it wasn't for Jayson, she might not be here.

She had eaten most of her breakfast before she managed to get words out again. "Tell me about your time in the service."

"I served in the Marine Corps and was a Harrier II pilot," he said. "Was in VMF 214 stationed in Yuma. We were known as the Black Sheep."

He went on, "I served and toured six years in Japan and was on the U.S.S. Tarawa."

When he'd given her the brief rundown of his background, he asked, "So, what about you? I know about your career, but not a whole lot more."

She hesitated, not really wanting to talk about herself, but what the hell. "I am an only child, born with a silver spoon in my mouth." She shrugged. "Mother is an only child, as is Father, so I don't have uncles and cousins. Just nannies and tutors, and one motherly cook. Not much more than that to tell."

"Did you ever go to public or private school?" he asked.

"My last four years were spent in a private school with girls who made me want to claw out my own eyes." Celine grimaced. "I had never seen so many vain, selfish, self-important girls in my life." She shook her head and laughed. "Myself excluded."

He raised an eyebrow.

"I had never been around other children," she said. "My parents frowned on people bringing over young kids." She hadn't thought about those years for some time now. "I pretty much lived in a museum of things they had collected. They probably thought of me as something they'd collected, but they didn't have the option to get rid of me. I couldn't touch anything and it was a cold, sterile environment."

She sighed and continued. "My parents had cocktail parties and banished me to my room. They didn't want me anywhere around, unless it was to use me as window dressing. When I was young, they would have my current nanny put me in a pretty outfit and have her make sure my curls were perfect. When they had a client with children, they brought me out to show off what great parents they were. Not because they actually cared about me."

She stared at her mug as images whirled through her mind. "As I grew older, it became based on my accomplishments. I still had to look exceptional, with perfect clothing and perfect hair, and I was required to have perfect manners. I also had to have perfect grades, shoot perfectly in both archery and with a rifle, and—" She almost said *ride* perfectly, but managed to stop herself in time. "That is not the world I would raise a child in. I wouldn't know what to do with a child if you had one here. I would just have no clue."

"Would you want kids if the circumstances were different?" he asked.

She thought about it as she looked up at him. "I don't know that I'd make a good mother. How could I if I don't know the slightest thing about little beings that are entirely dependent on the parent or caregiver? I've never even had a puppy or a kitten." She shook her head. "And I refuse to let tutors and nannies do the job for me. So, I guess the answer is no."

Celine shifted in her chair and finished her oatmeal. She really didn't want to talk anymore about her childhood or having children of her own. She'd decided long ago that she wasn't going to bring children into a world that considers a child to be window dressing.

Before she could change the topic from her life, Jayson asked, "What do your parents do now?"

"Whatever they feel like," Celine said. "They're incredibly wealthy, they're retired, and they travel the world. I see them at an occasional holiday or they pop in and visit me in New York if they happen to be in the city. I think it's more of a duty to them, than because they want to."

Saying the words hurt more than she ever thought they would. They seemed to wrap around her glass heart, squeezing until she thought it might shatter.

Her eyes ached as if she might cry.

She never cried. Why would she now?

Maybe it was the stabbing sensation in her head, the exhaustion from the ordeal…yes, that must have weakened her enough to get to this point.

She was a strong woman, and she didn't lean on men. She didn't lean on *anyone.*

But she was now...

Yes, definitely had to be the exhaustion and the ordeal.

"Do you have any pain killers?" She folded her hands on the tabletop. Strangely they were shaking. "Nothing strong, just enough to take the edge off the pain."

"I'll get you some ibuprofen." He got up from the table. "I should have asked when you came in."

He wasn't gone long, but it was enough that she had time to repair the breach in her composure. She hadn't realized it had cracked as much as it had.

When Jayson returned, he gave her two tablets and a glass of water, and sat facing her again.

Celine popped the tablets, chased them down with the water, then cleared her throat. "To be honest, I never faced the fact that my parents' failure to be good parents hurt as much as it does. I've made a lot of excuses for them, but ultimately, they really sucked as parents."

Before he could ask her more, she pressed forward. "Tell me about yours. Do you have pictures?"

"Sure, I've got pictures." Jayson pushed aside his coffee mug, then got to his feet. "Come into the family room."

She eased out of her chair, wincing from her sore muscles and bruises, and walked with him out of the kitchen and into a room filled with brown leather, roughhewn furniture, and art similar to that in his bedroom.

"My family isn't perfect, but they're good folks." He appeared to be thinking on his word choice as he walked to a large stone fireplace at one end of the room. "My family wasn't particularly well off, but we did okay. Better as we grew older."

They reached the fireplace and he gestured to a picture of himself, an older couple, and three younger men who looked a lot like Jayson, and a young woman. "This picture is from a year ago at Christmas." He pointed out the older couple. "My parents, Gus and Lissa." He indicated a man who looked a lot like him. "My fraternal twin brother, Jack, and my two younger brothers, Justice and James. The baby is our sister, Bailey."

Celine smiled. "Bailey isn't such a baby."

He shook his head and grinned. "Unfortunately, no. We have to keep the shotguns loaded."

"Poor girl." Celine laughed. "She doesn't stand a chance."

"Pretty much," he said with a grin.

"Sounds like you have the total opposite of my upbringing." Celeste caressed the side of the portrait. "To be honest, I envy you."

"I consider myself fortunate," he said. "The McBrides are all over this county and in Prescott in particular. Our upbringings couldn't be more different. Giant Easter egg hunts for the kids and tag football for the adults. Crazy Halloween parties and big Christmases."

He shook his head and gave a half-smile. "The McBrides do everything big around here." He nodded to more pictures on the mantel and on an old-fashioned upright piano. "Lots of ranchers, rodeo stars, the sheriff, a police officer, a detective, a private investigator, and a firefighter. And we've got babies and kids coming out our ears."

The image made her smile. Still, she shook her head, not able to picture herself in his situation, living a life like his. "I can't imagine having a family on that scale. I didn't even have grandparents around, much less siblings and cousins."

"There are some feuds here and there, some arguments pop up now and then, and we have the usual kinds of things families go through," he said. "But in the end, we're family."

"I wouldn't know what to do with one if I had one." She shook her head. "Poor little rich girl, right?"

He settled his hand on her shoulder. "Everyone deserves a family who cares for and loves them, blood or no. Parents who are there for them every step of their childhood. Not living in a museum, raised by other people, and used as window dressing. You deserved better."

She needed to turn attention away from herself. She moved to the upright piano.

"Bull riding, huh?" Celine bent to look at one of the framed photos on the piano. "You had a death wish?"

Jayson grinned. "My first rodeo was at the county fair, a hell of a long time ago. My cousin Creed dared me."

"You mentioned him." Celine gave him an amused look. "So, he was the instigator?"

"Can't say he had to push me." Jayson had a spark in his eye of amusement. "We both got cocky after sneaking into a popular, crowded saloon and not doing so bad on the mechanical bull. We were kicked out, but not until we'd each had a good ride."

"And when you got on a real bull at the fair?" Celine's lips tipped at the corners. "I suppose you were a natural?"

He snorted out a laugh. "Landed on my ass in the first second and broke my arm. Damned lucky the rodeo clowns got that bull off me or I'd have had more than that as a souvenir."

She winced. "I can't believe that didn't scare you off."

He shook his head. "Hell, no. I caught the bug and I caught it bad. Went on to compete for another six years."

"Yikes." She blew out her breath. "And all those broken bones you so proudly told me about earlier." She glanced at a photo of another man on the back of a bull. "Is that your cousin?"

"Yep." Jayson gave a quick nod. "Creed went on to become world champion a few times over."

"And you?" She folded her arms and leaned her hip against the piano. "Did you go far?"

"Nah." Jayson shook his head. "Had a good run, but Creed excelled in every way you could think of. Poetry in motion on the back of a bull."

"Not exactly what comes to mind when I think of poetry." She shifted her hip. "I'll take your word for it."

Jayson nodded at the photo she had first pointed out. "Some of the best years of my life were spent in rodeo arenas at county fairs." His expression went thoughtful, his gaze somewhere else. "I can still hear the crowd, smell the carnival scents mixed with manure. Colorful flags flapping and snapping in the breeze. Music pounding in between each ride before the next bull and rider are in the chute…"

He tapped his finger on the piano by the photo. "There's nothing like the roar of a crowd right before the quiet as the chute opens and the eight second ride begins."

Lightning flashed outside the windows, followed by an immediate crack of thunder.

"That strike was a close one," she said as she stared out the living room window. She'd been so into their conversation that she hadn't noticed that it had grown darker outside with a growing storm.

Rain drummed on the roof in a furious beat. More lightning flashed and more thunder boomed.

"I sure wish we would have known about this being your monsoon season." She shook her head. "We wouldn't be anywhere close right now."

The moment she said the words, she wasn't sure they were true. If it wasn't for the season, she wouldn't be with this man, having poured out her heart and realizing just how vulnerable she was—something she would never have believed just a day ago. Was that a good thing?

"And that Mercedes of yours wouldn't be at the bottom of an arroyo," he said. "Rented or not."

Celine shook her head. "It was rented. Regardless, it's just a thing, a possession. I'm happy to be alive."

"That makes two of us, honey," he said. "I was so damned worried for you. I'm glad you're feeling better."

"I am." She smiled. "Thanks to you."

"I've got to check on my pregnant mare," he said. "Would you like to go with me?"

She hesitated before nodding. "Yes." She grasped the neckline of her robe. "I seem to have ruined Bailey's clothes that you loaned me, not to mention mine are in a suitcase now under water. Do you have anything else I can borrow?"

"Yep." He nodded. "Come on into my bedroom. I'm bound to have something you can wear."

"Thanks." She kept her hands on the robe, holding it tightly so she didn't inadvertently flash him. She wasn't sure he would mind, but nevertheless, she preferred not to.

Although it might be fun under different circumstances.

When they reached his room, he dug through his drawers and found a pair of gray sweats and a T-shirt that would be baggy on her.

At first they were at a loss for shoes. Bailey's feet were smaller than Celine's, so her athletic shoes and western boots were too small. Jayson's feet were considerably larger.

"I can go barefoot," she said.

He frowned. "If you're going to be around horses, you need something on your feet."

She wanted to tell him she didn't need to be with the horses, but he didn't seem inclined to agree with her.

"I know what might work." He went to the guest room and returned with a pair of rubber boots. "Bailey uses these to muck out the stalls, and they just might fit." He handed them to her. "I can't let you in with the horses if you don't have decent shoes."

*I have no problem with that, she thought. No problem at all.*

Celine followed him through the house. Lightning illuminated the sky outside the windows, thunder only a couple of seconds behind.

"On second thought, stay in the house," he said as they entered the kitchen. "The storm is too close now."

"No. I want to go with you," she said. Maybe she should accept it as a blessing since she hadn't wanted to be around the horses, but she felt she *needed* to be with him. And the storm sort of scared the crap out of her. No, it *definitely* scared the crap out of her.

They were halfway across the kitchen when a tremendous bolt of lightning lit up the dark rain-filled morning. Thunder crashed at the same time, so loud it hurt her ears.

An explosion followed, the sound ripping through her like nothing she'd ever felt before.

She screamed threw herself in Jayson's arms, terror ripping through her. *The storm. The flood. The lightning. The thunder.* She heard it all, felt it all, in that instance.

The lights went out. The refrigerator stopped humming. Silence, save for the storm outside.

Thirty seconds later the appliances and lights came back on.

"What was that explosion?" She couldn't stop the catch in her voice as Jayson held her.

"It's okay, honey." Jayson hugged her. "I think the lightning got the transformer. The generator kicked on a few seconds after the power went out. We'll be fine with the generator for a while if necessary."

He added, "We'll have to pray that the explosion doesn't start a fire. The land is dry as hell right now."

He went to the window. It was still early in the day, but the storm made it appear as if it was already close to the night.

Lightning turned the dark sky into day. Thunder followed, but not as closely, and definitely not as loud.

Yet another flash of lightning, but farther away this time. Celine counted the seconds in her head before thunder boomed. "Five seconds. That lightning strike was a mile away."

He nodded. "I'll hold off going outside a little longer, until the storm is farther out."

When the thunder was a good ten seconds away, a distant rumble across the valley, Jayson looked out the window again.

"I'm going out to check on my mare." He pulled his phone out of his jeans pocket and went to an app that immediately showed views from multiple cameras. He selected one and an image of a horse lying down in a stall filled the screen. "It looks like Shiloh is foaling." He closed the app and tucked the phone back into his pocket.

He grabbed a heavy-duty flashlight from a shelf near the back door. "It'll be dark on the way to the barn."

She moved closer to him. "What if the power doesn't come on for a while?"

"The backup generators will last a while. I have one in the barn as well as the house, so we'll be fine for a few days. I have to keep them around thanks to storms like this one, and we can get isolated if the road is out."

"Good to know we're covered." She shivered from a chill that rolled over her body. Something about being isolated set her on edge. "Do you have another flashlight?" she asked.

He grabbed a smaller LED flashlight and handed it to her. "I need you to stay close."

*She took it. Not a problem.*

He plucked a beat-up western hat from off the hat tree. He selected a smaller one and put it on her head. It must have been Bailey's, because it fit her.

Thor joined them as they headed outside.

# CHAPTER 7

Rain continued to fall, but the storm itself was gone. Even though she wore rubber boots, Celine did her best to stay out of mud puddles. The one she'd found herself in was experience enough.

Celine's heart twisted when they reached the barn. It had been so long, and she'd managed quite well to avoid barns and horses altogether.

Now here she was, the last place she wanted to be.

Thor stood back as Jayson swung open the door and she followed his flashlight's beam with her own. Smells, familiar smells, brought back waves of memories. Alfalfa and sweet oats, alongside the smells of manure and horses.

The bittersweet memories were overshadowed by one so powerful it made her stomach churn. She nearly doubled over from the pain.

Jayson went to a stall and peered above the gate. He glanced over his shoulder at Celine, his face in shadows. "Shiloh seems to be doing well."

Despite the twisting in her gut every time she was close to a horse, she approached the stall.

"I'm going to stay in the barn," he said, "and watch her on the camera to make sure there are no issues. The vet won't be able to get here if we need her."

Celine peeked over the stall door, and saw a beautiful brindle mare who was on her side, her side rising and falling in a rapid movement, and her breathing coming faster than it should.

"She's distressed," Celine said.

"Probably the storm." Jayson said. "One of the reasons why I don't want to be too far from her.

"I'll stay with you," Celine said.

He took off his western hat, water still dripping from it. He made sure the mare's stall was dimmer than the rest of the barn. He told her horses preferred the dark or dim lighting when they were foaling.

Other horses whickered softly and shifted in their stalls. All seemed calm.

He sat on an alfalfa hay bale at the bottom of a huge stack of bales, and gestured for her to join him. She did, and Thor made himself comfortable on the ground at Celine's feet.

Jayson held up his phone with his gaze on the horse as she breathed in and out, her sides like bellows.

Celine watched until Jayson closed out the app. She leaned her head back against the side of the mountain of hay bales. She closed her eyes and let the smells, sounds, and the presence of horses wash over her.

The pain of loss and guilt weighed so heavy on her that she thought she might sink through the barn floor. If it wasn't for her, the beautiful and proud Arabian she had loved so much would have lived a long and pleasant life.

Celine swallowed past the giant lump lodged in her throat and opened her eyes.

Jayson watched her, his face partially shadowed in the glow of the lights he'd set up in the stall.

"What's on your mind?" Jayson's question shouldn't have startled her, but it still caught her off guard.

"Just memories." She shook her head. "Old memories."

He put his forearms on his knees, and he said what she hadn't had the courage to. "Hard memories."

She wrapped her arms around her bent knees. "Yeah, you could say that."

"You used to be around horses and you were close to them." His assessment caused her to widen her eyes. Was she that transparent?

She looked away from him. "Yes."

"Celine, what happened?" He spoke in that gentle soothing voice that unraveled her.

She closed her eyes and pictured the golden Arabian.

"She was so beautiful." Celine felt tears prick at the backs of her eyes, but she refused to cry. She didn't deserve to feel one bit sorry for herself.

She opened her eyes and met Jayson's gaze. "Her name was Golden Knight Sky."

"What did you call her?" Jayson asked.

"Sky." Celine smiled. "I was fifteen when my parents bought her for me. She was a palomino Arabian, but some thought she was an Akhal-Teke because her mane and tail were like liquid gold, and her coat rippled in the sunshine in a slightly deeper shade."

Celine leaned her head back on the stall door. "I loved her for her personality. She was proud and carried herself as if she knew she was beautiful. I think she did know that." Celine smiled at the memory of Sky prancing around an arena. "Her personality sparkled like her coat, and she was sweet and loving. As you know, I had no human friends. But I had Sky and she was everything to me."

"You showed her?" Jayson asked.

"More than that." Celine pressed her shoulders back. "We

competed in dressage, show jumping, and other events. We were unstoppable."

Jayson never took his eyes off her. "What happened to Sky?"

Celine had known the question was coming, but it still jarred her.

She looked away, unable to meet Jayson's eyes. "My parents allowed me to attend a private school for what you would consider my high school years." Celine clenched her fists on her thighs. "I made friends. Sort of. But it was a different feeling for me. A sense of belonging with other people when I'd never belonged."

Celine shook her head. "Or so I thought I belonged." She brushed that comment away with a wave of her hand. "I'd always been so good at taking care of Sky. I *loved* her." Celine managed to keep back the tears. "But I started to get lazy. Every now and then I would get invited to a girls' party, and if I was running late, I would leave Sky for Ralph, our stable boy, to put up and feed."

Celine clenched her fists tighter, digging her fingernails into her palms. The pain was nothing compared to what churned inside.

"One night I couldn't wait to go to a sleepover. I wanted to go and giggle with the girls about boys and whatever, even though I had no experience. I just laughed and pretended I did.

"That night, one of father's disgruntled former employees, poisoned the feed in the barn I'd left her in for Ralph to put away." Celine clenched her jaws so tightly together pain shot through her head. "Sky was given the poisoned feed. She died that night."

The pain, the horror, the guilt—all of it nearly sent Celine into a tailspin.

*I don't deserve to feel anything but guilt.*

"It was my fault she died." She couldn't look at Jayson at all and she stared instead at the brindle mare. "If I had put her back where she belonged…"

She shook her head, unable to continue.

Jayson settled his arm over her shoulders. She hadn't even noticed he had moved close to her. She remained stiff in his half-embrace

"Relax," he said.

"I don't deserve to feel comforted." The words were almost too thick to get out.

"Shhh." Jayson pulled her closer. "You've carried this guilt far too long. It wasn't your fault. The ex-employee could have targeted the other barn. You could have done everything perfectly and she still could have died."

"No." Celine shook her head. "She would have lived."

Jayson said nothing, just held her to him.

She tried to remain frozen in his arms, but the fight for her own life in the arroyo had taken its toll.

*How can I seek comfort after nearly dying, when Sky did die?*

But her body wouldn't listen. She was too exhausted to do anything. She sank against Jayson and rested her head on his shoulder.

"Good girl," he said.

"I'm not one of your horses," she said. "I'm not an innocent. I might as well have killed Sky myself."

"Shhh." Was he rocking her now?

It was a gentle motion that lulled her into sinking into him.

"We all have regrets, Celine," he said softly. "Some bigger than others. We would go back and change those things if we could. But that can't happen. At least not with loss of life. But we can do other things."

He continued to rock her lightly, and she continued to listen, even though she didn't think anything he said would make a difference.

"Horses are healing, Celine. You know that. Let them heal you.

Celine considered his words. "Maybe." She blew out her

breath. "I don't know if I can heal, but you're right. They have a magic, a power inside that can take someone broken and make them whole again."

"Yes." Jayson touched her chin with his fingertip. "And you can start with you."

They spent the rest of the evening in the barn, sometimes talking, sometimes silent. Celine didn't mind the silence, it allowed her to turn things over in her mind.

Was Jayson right? Was it time she let go and allow herself to heal?

"World meet baby. Baby meet world." Jayson showed her the barn camera app and she grinned. He exited the app and stuffed his phone in his pocket. "You can watch over the stall door if you'd like."

"I definitely would like to." Celine got up with him from their seat on the hay.

Jayson grabbed a couple of things he'd gathered ahead of time and took them into the stall with him before closing the door. Celine put her forearms on the top rail and watched.

"You did yourself proud, Shiloh," Jayson said as he crouched beside the baby and her mama. "She's a beauty."

Shiloh snuffled her agreement.

Jayson checked the baby over, dipped the umbilical cord in iodine, and made sure the foal stood and ate as soon as it was ready.

He glanced over his shoulder and smiled at Celine.

She stared at the baby with wonder. "She has such tiny, perfect hooves and her fuzzy little body is so adorable." Celine couldn't help but smile as she watched the baby feed from her mother. "The love and dedication of the mother horse is precious and wonderful, and so powerful."

"What would be a good name for her?" Jayson asked Celine.

The sweet baby was gorgeous. "Sierra."

"Sierra." Jayson looked thoughtful then nodded. "That's a good name for this little girl."

When mother and baby were settled for the night, Jayson and Celine walked back to the house. He would check in on the pair with the camera app every now and then, but for now all looked good.

"That was amazing." She smiled at Jayson. "Thank you for including me." She felt a little shy as she added, "And thank you for our talk tonight."

"Anytime." He draped his arm around Celine's shoulders and they walked together to the ranch house. "And I mean that."

She smiled up at him. She barely knew him, but the way he kept her close felt right and comfortable.

The power came on just after they got back to the house. Celine was drained from the long day. Her body had been through so much and she hadn't had a chance to fully heal.

"I'm exhausted." She gave him a tired smile. "We can swap rooms and I can give you back yours."

"Stay in my room. I'm fine in the guest room." Jayson hugged her as if they'd known each other forever. Wonderful heat filled her body from the way his big, powerful arms made her feel. "Sweet dreams, Celine," he said as he released her.

*Wow. Just Wow.* All she could do was nod and say, "Good night," before she turned and walked down the hallway.

If her dreams included anything that made her feel the way he'd just made her body sing, she would have very sweet dreams indeed.

THE NEXT DAY, Celine began to feel like herself again. She was still incredibly sore, but she wasn't as tired and she had more energy.

She reached the kitchen and Thor greeted her. "You're such a good boy," she said. She crouched to scratch him behind his ears.

The smell of coffee and something delicious met her nose. Jayson was there, as he always seemed to be at six-thirty in the morning. He was off doing chores by five and finished by then.

Celine smiled and got up from her crouch. Thor retreated to his pillow by the refrigerator as she walked toward Jayson. The tile felt cool beneath her bare feet, his robe brushing the tops of her feet. She liked being in his robe. He'd said he never wore it, but she could swear his scent was in the soft terry cloth.

Jayson offered her a mug of hot, steaming coffee before she'd even had a chance to say two words. "Good morning, beautiful."

He said it so naturally, as if they'd known each other forever. What sounded like an endearment warmed her from head to toe, and she didn't mind one bit.

The man radiated strength and intelligence, a heady combo. He wore a black T-shirt that fit him oh-so-well, Wrangler jeans that she knew hugged a tight ass, and boots that looked as if they fit him like a glove and that he'd had forever. She'd never felt desire like she felt around this man. The days she'd spent with Jayson had made her wonder if the log hitting her head had done some damage. She barely knew the man and he made her feel like she belonged with him.

*Celine, pull it together, she told herself.*

She reached him and took the mug of coffee. She inhaled and sighed with pleasure. "Best. Smell. Ever."

"Almost." He looked at her in a way that made her feel as if he'd just made love to her. Sexy. Hot. Passionate. But caring and loving and—

*Dear God.*

Her cheeks grew hot and she drew the knot on the robe tighter. "How's the road?"

Jayson shook his head. "Still too much rain in the mountains for the county to fix that canyon of a crossing."

She sipped her coffee. "Is water still in the arroyo?"

"It's been running non-stop thanks to the tremendous

amount of rain we're getting in the mountains." He leaned his hip against the counter, his mug in one hand. "We haven't had rain like this in a decade. Our neck of the woods is saying a great big thank you to the heavens."

She sipped again and felt peace coming back to her body and brain. "I'm glad it's good for you. It's not something I've ever had to worry about."

Jayson tipped his head back and finished the last of his mug before lowering it. "It's too bad it's messing up your schedule."

"It's only money." She gave a wry smile. "The way it's been going out the window, what's ten or twenty grand more?"

He winced. "Ow."

"Feel free to say that again." She shook her head. "Accounting issues, ransomware, expenses, blah, blah, blah."

"Ransomware?" He frowned. "Are you talking about what's in the news? According to CNN, the hackers mostly went after big companies as well as hospitals and government agencies, mostly outside the U.S."

Celine tilted her head to the side. "They must have gone for some small businesses, too. Monty said they got me pretty badly. Twenty-thousand dollars."

Jayson looked thoughtful then poured himself another cup of coffee.

She tipped her mug and stared at the bottom. "I'm on empty, too. All this talk means I'll need a whole carafe to myself."

He poured her another mug. "I'm sorry to hear you got hit."

"Me, too." She moved to the kitchen table and sat. "Monty is taking care of it all. Before the attack, he said I have enough money for this and the launch with room to spare. I hope that still holds." She breathed in the warm smell coming from the direction of the oven. "Tell me that's breakfast."

"I threw together some egg, cheese, bacon, and sausage omelet muffins." He glanced at the timer on the stove. "Three minutes, but I'll check on them."

He grabbed a potholder and opened the oven door. "They're ready. Your nose is right on the button."

"Yummy." She left her mug on the table and went to the cabinet to get breakfast plates, then grabbed forks and napkins.

Jayson took out a small platter and loaded it with the omelet muffins. "Enough to feed a small army and have leftovers, too."

Celine smiled as she got salsa and sour cream out of the fridge. She couldn't help smiling around Jayson.

When everything was on the table, they dug in.

"This is so freaking good." Celine gave a little groan of pleasure after her first bite. "You can cook for me anytime you'd like. Day or night." She looked at him with a teasing look. "Oh, yeah. You *have* been cooking for me day and night. I owe you a few meals."

"Do you cook?" Jayson asked.

She hadn't been well enough to even think of it until now. She gave him a dead-serious look. "I have a phone and I know how to use it."

He grinned, and she went on. "Seriously though, I can make a few things. Enough that I don't starve when I'm on my own. And there's nothing on speed dial."

"No delivery here." He inclined his head toward the pantry. "I have plenty of rations."

"Now there's a word I haven't heard for a while."

THE DAY WAS clear with a clean rain-washed scent as Celine walked out to the barn.

When they'd finished breakfast, they had taken care of the dishes. Jayson left, riding Starlight to check on things around his property, like fence lines and water troughs. He'd asked Celine if she wanted to go and she had declined. Thor was gone with Jayson.

Jayson had said he could be gone a couple of hours, or most of the day, depending on what waited for him out there.

She wasn't sure why she was drawn to the barn this morning.

*Melting.* She was melting...and falling in love with his horses.

Her breath caught in her throat and she came to a complete stop.

"No." She shook her head. "I can't fall in love with his horses. I won't."

She should run back to the house and never enter the barn again. It was a dishonor to Sky's memory.

Or was it a dishonor to Sky's memory to have turned her back on that world altogether?

Sky was a horse...but she'd been more than that. Proud, beautiful, intelligent.

Celine forced her feet to move and keep walking to the barn. Sky had been her confidant. Celine had spilled her heart and soul to that wonderful, precious being. She'd had no friends, and hadn't been allowed to socialize with "strangers." Which meant she was entirely alone, because everyone had been a stranger. So how could she have any friends?

Not that her parents cared.

For the most part, she'd come to terms with who her parents were, and her upbringing. But sometimes—sometimes she felt that little girl loneliness and pain, an ache deep in her soul.

She reached the barn door and grasped the handle that felt cool to the touch.

She stood in the open barn doorway, listening to the sounds of the morning. Cattle lowed in the field and horses whickered in the corral.

It was the soft sounds the horses made that did it.

Tears burned the backs of her eyes and her throat filled with a solid ball of pain.

Over fifteen years. She'd held back every single tear since she'd walked away.

She had refused to cry when Sky was poisoned. That same day she turned her back on the world she had known and loved.

A world that had been everything to her, because of Sky.

She had refused to ever acknowledge it again.

Now, as she looked at the robin's egg blue of the morning sky, everything quieted and she thought she heard the whisper of butterfly wings. Soft. A faintness that brushed her heart.

She raised her chin and pushed the barn door all the way open, letting in the morning sunlight. Her heart thumped a little harder as she walked to the horse stalls. The other horses were outside in the corral and Jayson was off riding Starlight. Celine was alone with Shiloh and Sierra.

Celine looked over the stall door.

Shiloh walked up to the door.

Sierra peeked out from behind her mother.

Celine's heart pounded. She wanted to turn, leave, never come back to the barn. She was dishonoring Sky.

*You're honoring Sky.*

Celine's fingertips trembled until they met the coarse hair on Shiloh's nose. An immediate connection, like a golden rope, shot through her hand and straight to her heart.

The power of it nearly sent Celine staggering backward. She managed to maintain her footing.

She closed her eyes and held her fingers to Shiloh's face, not daring to do anything. She wished she could go into the stall, but with Sierra in there, Shiloh would probably be protective and not want Celine near the baby.

The horse stepped closer so that her head was over the stall door. Celine raised her eyelids and looked at her. Shiloh's big, intelligent brown eyes returned her gaze.

Celine wrapped her arms around Shiloh's neck and pressed her face against the horse's coarse hair. She breathed in the smell of horse.

She'd loved that smell. It brought back so many memories.

The times she and Sky had ridden, free of any constraints. The times they practiced, competed, and won.

But most of all, she remembered moments like this, when she was hugging Sky, not wanting to leave. She'd wanted to stay and feel the unconditional love between them.

Celine drew back and looked at Shiloh. The horse whickered and bobbed her head. Her big soulful eyes seemed to say, "It's okay. Everything is okay."

Tears, fifteen years of tears flooded from her. They rolled down her face as her throat opened and she let out the pain in every sob. She didn't hold back. Didn't want to hold back. It had been too long and she didn't think she could ever stop.

Her tears lessened and the chain around her heart snapped.

She braced her forehead against Shiloh's, feeling the short hair against her skin.

"Thank you," she whispered. "Thank you."

JAYSON RETURNED from his ride on Starlight, bone weary and hungry as hell.

He brushed down the mare, fed her, and did other evening chores before heading into the house with Thor.

The moment he walked into the kitchen from the back porch, heavenly smells hit him square in the face.

Celine stood at the stove, her back to him. She looked over her shoulder when he closed the door and she smiled.

Damn, but she had a sexy smile. A welcoming smile.

"Great timing," she said. "It'll be ready in about fifteen minutes."

He tossed his Stetson onto the hat tree. "Smells downright incredible."

She laughed. "Let's see how you like it once you taste it."

He took the time to watch her as she grabbed a potholder off the countertop. She wore Bailey's jeans that he'd run through the washer twice. The Wranglers fit Celine's well-shaped ass perfectly. She had on one of his T-shirts that she'd tied off to the side. This morning he'd noticed how the soft material hugged her breasts, like he wanted to do right now.

Her back was to him as she said, "You have time to get cleaned up."

He held back a grin. "That bad, huh?"

She faced him, a wooden spoon in one hand, a potholder in the other. "You tell me."

He raised his hands. "I will get my tail end into the shower and be back within fifteen minutes."

"Good boy." She bent to open the oven, that ass of hers looking delicious enough to forget what he was supposed to be doing.

Oh, hell, he *had* forgotten.

With that image of her in his mind, he headed for the shower.

Fourteen minutes later—who was counting—he was in the kitchen.

"You're back." She nodded to the plates and utensils. "Do you mind setting the table?"

"Sure thing." He'd do anything to get a bite of whatever she'd made. Hell, he'd probably do anything for her.

She gave him the once over. "You sure do clean up good."

This time he did grin. "As instructed, ma'am."

She sniffed. "I'm too young to be a ma'am. Don't you have to be at least forty?"

"Nah." He shook his head. "Us country boys call every lady ma'am from the time they're in high school 'til they're a hundred."

She smiled. "In that case, it's okay." She went back to stirring a big pan of pasta, with a dark creamy-looking sauce. Nearby was a baking sheet with crusty bread on it.

"What's for dinner?" he asked as she turned off the heat from beneath the pan. "I recognize the bread, but not whatever smells so good in that pan."

"Beef Bolognese." She looked at him. "Trivet?"

"What?" He felt momentarily like she'd thrown him a curveball. Then it clicked. "Oh, one of those things." He pulled one out of a drawer. "Never had Bolognese. Can't wait to try it."

She took the trivet. "You have an amazing amount of supplies in your pantry and freezer. I never expected that on a ranch."

He raised a brow. "You imagined pinto beans, cornbread, and beef stew?"

"Um." She paused then laughed. "Well, yeah."

"I have a new cook." His stomach rumbled. "She's excellent and has been keeping me and the boys well-fed."

"Nice." Celine took the trivet, a serving spoon, and a spoon rest to the table and set it all on the surface.

Jayson picked up the pan of Bolognese and placed it on the trivet at the middle of the table.

"We're also having spinach salad." She went to the fridge and pulled out a large bowl. "With homemade bleu cheese dressing."

He seated himself at the table after she was settled. "Something is in the oven."

"Dessert." She gave him a mischievous look. "I just put it in before you returned from your shower. You'll have to wait and see what it is."

Jayson shook his head. This woman never ceased to amaze him.

He filled both their plates and then he dug in. "Holy cow, this is good."

Her smile broadened. "Thank you."

He shoveled in another mouthful, chewed and swallowed. "Keep this up and I won't let you out of the kitchen."

"As much fun as this has been, I am going to have to get back to work." She knitted her brows. "I checked Monty's trailer earlier today and I still can't find my tote with my laptop and some important papers."

Jayson frowned. "You're sure you left it there?"

"Positive." She nodded. "It was the same morning we met. I went into the trailer, threw my purse and tote on the couch, and searched for the coffee. That was the last time I saw it."

Jayson studied her. "Do you think someone could have stolen it?"

"I don't know." She sighed. "I like to think we can trust all our people. They're vetted. They go through background checks, we require three references, and we query credit sources, yadda, yadda, yadda. I've had nothing but the highest regard for any of them." She made an expression of frustration. "Charlie is a big pain in the ass, but I don't think he'd steal. He's got Monty buying him things like $5,000 drones. Why would he take my laptop?"

"It's a shame, but I suppose you never know completely about people," Jayson said. "We'll just hope someone set it aside a little too much out of the way."

She gave a self-deprecating laugh before she went on. "And then there's the tote. I paid as much for it as I did for the laptop, if not more. I have to say, not one of my better purchases. I have enjoyed it, but I spent way too much on the thing."

"I think we should take a look for your bag and laptop tomorrow." Jayson glanced outside. "Another storm is building up, and I hear thunder."

"I agree." She stared out the big kitchen window, too. "I really need to catch a break, and soon."

## CHAPTER 8

Revenge. Yes...nothing tasted better.

Monty narrowed his eyes as he looked at Celine's login screen. "What is her damned password?"

He needed it *now*.

Monty ground his teeth. Her father, Charles Northland, had taken everything from him. It was only fitting that he should regain his wealth by robbing Northland's daughter.

The purse he would have won with his horse would have gone toward MERF. But not only was Monty unable to run his horse in the race, thanks to that cheating sonofabitch Northland, Monty's horse, who he'd run under the name of Merf's Dream, had to be put down.

Monty had sunk everything into that damned horse, and had ended up with *nothing*.

Fucking Northland.

Monty might not be able to touch the bastard, but he'd put himself in line to get everything from Celine. He had full access to all her business accounts. Now he just needed her passwords to take everything from the accounts her parents had set up for her. Celine refused to use the money from her parents because she wanted to "make it on her own."

*Yeah, right.* Just being a Northland got her places she wouldn't have made it to before.

And her clothing line—he already had a buyer who would pay through the nose for Celine's designs.

Who knew why? What was that crap women wore today? Hell, women should all be home taking care of their husbands. His parents' generation and the generations before that had it right.

Maybe her password was the date he'd killed her horse. He still remembered the exact day. He remembered everything about it.

He punched in the date and growled when it didn't work.

Monty remembered seeing her as a snot-nosed brat, riding that horse like she was some kind of freaking princess. That her horse got caught up in Monty's revenge—well, it couldn't have been helped. And as demanding and bitchy as she'd appeared to be, she'd deserved it.

And now—well, even though she didn't know it, she was paying for his farm in Belize. He'd just put a bid on it and knew it would be his. The property had been sitting for a while, but he really didn't care about that.

He'd never be found there. Never. And he'd have peace, solitude, with only the servants to take care of him and otherwise stay silent. A small town with modern conveniences was close, but not close enough to bother him.

The collection of twenty-one different tropical birds the former owner had left behind—whipped cream on the sundae.

"Now I need to get those fucking passwords." He stared at her laptop's login screen and the blinking cursor in the password box. Apparently, he'd have to get to Celine and make her give them to him.

He just had to figure out *how.*

Monty pushed aside Celine's laptop and turned to his desktop computer. He glanced at his handwritten notes lying beside the keyboard, and picked them up. He'd called a few companies specializing in blocking ransomware attacks, and he knew exactly what to do to set up his own software protection company—on paper—so that he could shovel more of Celine's money into it.

He had become so good at doing that exact thing with a handful of other "companies." Once he disappeared, it would take them a good long time to unravel it—and he'd made sure they'd never know everything.

Best of all, he would be gone, where they would never think to look for him. On farmland in the rainforest of Belize, fifty acres of peace all around him in the foothills of the Maya Mountains, he'd live the life he deserved.

Yeah, Monty's Early Retirement Funds would soon be fat enough to finally do what he'd been dreaming about for years.

He opened his email program and waited for it to download messages into the account he used for Celine's business, those for the fake companies he'd set up, and then his private email—that was the important one.

Messages popped up in his inboxes, but it was the one in his private account that he went to first.

It was from his real estate agent, Maria, the subject line *Maya Mountain property.*

He didn't know why his stomach clenched. He clicked on the email.

Mr. Tinsman,

*I have been trying to reach you by telephone with no success. You have been outbid by another potential buyer. Their offer is $500,000 U.S. Would you like to bid higher?*

*There are many beautiful farms in Belize. However, I do not believe* *you will find another home quite like this one. I recommend $600,000 U.S.*

*Please advise,*
*Maria Fernanda Vasquez*

MONTY BALLED his fists and restrained himself from punching the monitor.

Someone had bid against him.

His muscles tightened and his head ached from how tightly he clenched his jaws.

All he had right now was half a million. He couldn't blow it all on the property without having the rest of Celine's money. He'd thought he had plenty of time.

Including investor funds, the crowd funding, and Celine's personal accounts, he'd have another one and a half million. He'd had to do it slowly, but this changed things.

He had to do it all *now*.

# CHAPTER 9

Celine raised her arms over her head, stretching her muscles. She'd just finished hand drying the baking dish she'd used to make her favorite casserole for lunch—a pasta dish that was the best comfort food ever.

"I could so use a massage." She sighed into the stretch. "It's been a week now, but my body still feels like I got hit by a car."

"You pretty much did." Jayson started the dishwasher. "I'd offer to give you a massage, but I'm afraid I'll hit some of those bumps and bruises and hurt you."

"Would you really give me one?" Celine perked up as she lowered her arms—it sounded too wonderful to pass up. "You won't hurt me. I will be more than fine."

"If you're sure." The low rumble of his words sent a thrill through her.

*Maybe this isn't such a good idea,* she thought as she met Jayson's gaze.

*Maybe it's the perfect idea.*

She dried her hands on a towel. "Where?"

He thought about it a moment. "One of the beds is the best I can do. Of the two guestrooms, one has a smaller mattress. That's the best place."

"Works for me." She walked with him to the hall outside the kitchen. "The sooner the better."

He took her to the opposite side of the house, where the guestrooms were. She hadn't been in either of them, but she knew the layout of his home after spending a week here.

"The smallest of the two rooms is the first on the right." He added, "I'll grab some lotion and meet you there."

"I'll be waiting," she said. Waiting and anxious.

He went back the way they came and vanished around a corner.

Celine wandered into the room. It was small and painted a pretty robin's egg blue with white curtains and white furniture. It could easily be a kid's room with the right décor. She could picture a big ol' Teddy bear on the bed, and children's toys all over the room.

As for her, she hadn't been allowed to have anything "common" as her parents had called kids' toys in stores like Toys 'R' Us. FAO Schwarz made the list of acceptable, but they rarely bought anything for her from the store.

No, they'd bought her porcelain dolls, huge handmade doll houses that included beautiful perfectly made furniture for her dolls, all commissioned just for her. However, she'd barely been allowed to play with them because they had been so expensive and so brilliantly made. That was just the tip of the iceberg of overly expensive, elite toys she'd been given as a child.

She shook her head. The thought of being a child made her think of the little girl who stomped on one of her papers, and Celine smiled. Funny how her perspective had changed so rapidly. She wasn't even sure why it had. If she had ever run away from her mother in an airport, she would have been locked in her room for a week. She hoped the little girl's mother was more understanding than that.

A rocking chair was tucked in one corner, and she kicked off the rubber boots and put them near it before stripping off her jeans. She didn't have a bra to worry about and she left the big T-shirt and panties on.

Celine took the pillows from the bed and set them on the rocking chair. She plopped on the comfortable mattress and arranged herself face down.

She closed her eyes and forced herself to relax and not think in a sexual way of the big man's hands on her body. She had to admit to herself she'd wanted that since the moment they'd met.

Of course, this would *only* be a massage.

If she had it her way, it would be more than that. The thought stilled her. Did she really want that from Jayson?

*Yes.* She swallowed as she admitted it to herself again. *Absolutely yes.*

Jayson's presence filled the room the moment he walked in. He sucked in his breath, like he hadn't expected her to take off the jeans.

She opened her eyes and met his. "I'm ready."

"I can see that." He stared at her as if she was completely naked, then shook it off before the three easy strides he took to get to the bed.

"I found lavender massage oil," he said. "My kid sister was going through some kind of scent therapy thing. She gave me a basket of stuff at Christmas and said the lavender oil is supposed to make me relax." He snorted. "I'd forgotten about it."

Celine wriggled on the bed." Lavender oil sounds perfect."

He glanced to the bottle, then to her. "If we're going to use the oil, you've got to lose that shirt."

"I definitely want that oil." She wriggled as he helped her pull off the T-shirt without exposing her breasts. He tossed the shirt onto the mound of pillows.

Now all she was wearing were her panties. Things were getting better.

A shiver trailed her spine as he squirted oil on her back.

"Too cold?" he asked.

The pleasant scent of lavender relaxed her and she closed her eyes. "Not at all."

The mattress dipped a little when he sat on the bed. She held her breath, waiting for his touch.

The moment his warm, strong hands were on her shoulders, she sighed with pleasure. "That feels so amazing."

"You've got quite a few bruises." He skimmed his fingers over her back. "I'll do my best to avoid them."

"Just put those wonderful hands to work." She sighed. "I'm already feeling better."

Jayson moved his hands to her shoulders and began kneading her tight muscles.

His touch was magic. Pure magic.

She'd had massages in exclusive spas all around the world. At this moment, she didn't think she'd ever had a massage as wonderful as Jayson's.

He worked his way slowly to her head and concentrated on her scalp and her neck.

His hands soothed and lulled her, working out not only aches and pains from the accident, but those from stress and worry from her life and her business.

She melted, feeling as if she might sink into the mattress.

The lavender oil filled her lungs, but Jayson's scent saturated her senses in a different way.

He kept his attention on her muscles, not touching her in a sexual manner. But she became more and more aware of him in every way possible.

Her nipples tightened, her breasts aching for his hands, his mouth. She barely held back a moan of pleasure and tried not to squirm from the tingles between her thighs.

Jayson slowed when he reached her hips. "How does that feel?"

His rumbling voice sent a shiver through her. "Amazing. Please don't stop." It probably sounded like she was begging, but she didn't care. She just wanted him to keep his hands on her.

"All right." He worked his fingers across her back. "You've still got plenty of knots in your muscles that I can work out."

"I can't tell you how much I appreciate this." She felt a little naughty as she slid her hand up her side and dragged her fingers along her skin just above the curve of her breast. "It's sore here."

He paused. "Then I'll have to take care of that."

She let out another sigh. "Mmm." He lightly massaged the skin where she had showed him.

She shifted just enough to the side that his hand slipped to her breast.

He stilled but didn't remove his hand then slowly skimmed her nipple with his thumb. "I take it you need a little massaging here?"

"Most definitely." She scooted onto her back and looked up at him, his hand still on her. "My breasts especially need attention."

"Oh, they do…" He let his voice trail off as he cupped her other breast and brushed her nipple with his fingertips. "What else do they need?"

Her voice came out low and husky. "Your mouth for starters."

HE STUDIED HER, his palm hot over her breast, the heat in his gaze burning her through. "You like to play with fire."

"Maybe." She put her hand over his, feeling the warmth of his skin next to hers.

"No maybe about it." He squeezed her nipple hard enough that she gasped. The sensation shot a thrill straight between her thighs.

Her throat worked as she stared up into his eyes. "What are you going to do about it?"

The corner of his mouth tipped into a sensual smile. "I like playing with fire, too." He lowered his head and nuzzled her hair. "Damn, you smell good. You always smell good."

She wasn't surprised he'd noticed. He'd been watching her since she'd been back on her feet, the same way she'd been watching him.

He slid his fingers into her hair and cupped the back of her head. He inhaled, a deep audible sound that ended with a groan.

"We shouldn't be doing this." The fight in his words told her how much he was struggling against it.

"Why?" she whispered.

"Damned if I know." He slid his lips over her cheek and captured her mouth with his.

She moaned as he slid his tongue into her mouth. She tasted his masculine flavor and breathed in his untamed scent. She could feel the flames between them ignite and burn hot.

The kiss was long, slow, and deep. He drew her in with that kiss, giving her more than she'd even dreamed of, her whole body now on fire.

He slid his lips from hers and trailed them along the curve of her neck to her throat.

"Jayson." His name came through her lips on a sigh.

A low growl rose in his throat, the rumble vibrating through her senses, stirring her arousal, making it grow even more.

He slipped her nipple into his hot mouth and she shuddered with pleasure. He sucked and she moaned and arched her back, wanting more of him and wanting him now.

"You're so damned sweet," he murmured as he moved his lips to her other nipple.

He hesitated, his warm breath fanning the taut nub. She whimpered and he flicked his tongue over her nipple.

She gasped, slid her fingers into his hair, and pulled his head in closer.

He drew her nipple into his mouth and sucked. She whimpered again as wild sensations rolled through her.

He moved his hand down her flat belly to the juncture between her thighs and beneath her panties. He dipped his finger into her wetness and stroked her clit.

She nearly came off the bed as she cried out. She needed the release only he could give her.

He sucked her nipple harder and she clenched her fist in his hair. She squirmed, wanting more of him.

Deep inside, she knew this man could satisfy her like no other.

He released her nipple and raised his head so that he met her gaze. "You shouldn't have started this."

"Why not?" She found it hard to breathe.

"Because with you, I'm not sure I can stop."

She slid her hand down to his cheek, his stubble rough beneath her palm. "I don't want you to stop."

"I gathered that." He gave her a slow, sensual smile. "But there are a whole lot of reasons why we should."

She scooted up in bed so that she could lean closer to him. "Give me an example."

"You nearly died out there." His expression sobered. "For all we know, you have a concussion and you're not thinking clearly."

"I am thinking clearly." She moved her hands to his chest, feeling the hard flesh beneath her palms. "I've had a concussion before, and I know I wouldn't feel close to wanting to do all that I can with you. I'm okay, Jayson, and I want you."

"You haven't known me long enough," he said quietly. "I think you need to."

She tipped her head to the side. "Why would that make a difference?"

"Because there are things about me that might make you change your mind and fast," he said.

"Unless you killed a man in cold blood, I can't imagine a reason that might make me think that way." She brushed her knuckles over his skin. "Why don't you try me?"

He stilled then shook his head. "Now isn't the place or time."

Celine frowned, not sure how to take his abrupt halt. Was he full of crap, and this was an excuse to break off what they had started?

Or did he genuinely have something he thought would make her change her mind? She couldn't imagine why he'd make up something like that.

Jayson got to his feet, his blue eyes appraising, his expression unreadable. "Why don't you get dressed, and I'll head on out. I need to ride the fence line with Starlight."

Now she did feel a chill from his abruptness.

Anger flashed inside her, hot and bright. But she refused to let him see it. She slipped off the bed and refused to look at him as she gathered her clothes and put them on.

"Celine—"

"Save it." She couldn't hold back her anger like she'd thought she'd be able to. "I have things to do, too. So go on your ride and I'll see you when I see you."

For a long moment, he studied her and didn't leave. She clenched her jaw and met his gaze. She could think of nothing to say, so she dodged past him, out of the room, and into the hall.

Celine strode toward his bedroom to gather what things she had. She'd stay in Monty's trailer before she'd spend another night in Jayson's home.

She reached Jayson's bedroom and put her hands on her hips. She blew out her breath. She had nothing to retrieve. Absolutely nothing. All she had were the borrowed clothes she was wearing, and she couldn't strip and walk out of there naked.

Well, she could, but it wasn't the optimal solution.

She ground her teeth and marched through the house, then outside. Thor appeared at her side—she wasn't sure where he'd been. She scratched him behind his ears. "Stay here, boy."

A soft rain was falling and she ignored it. She pushed her now curling hair out of her face. Her borrowed rubber boots squished in the mud and she watched her step. When she reached Monty's trailer, she climbed up the stairs, tugged off the dirty boots and set them by the doormat, and jerked the door open.

Celine shivered as she closed the door behind her and stepped into the dim interior of the trailer. She folded her arms across her chest as she looked around.

What a mess—and likely due to Charlie. He must have come in after she'd shot down the drone and kicked things around because he was pissed.

Well, he should have listened to her to begin with, when she told him to keep the damned thing away from the shoot.

She plopped down in front of a computer desk. The only thing on it was an expensive-looking laptop that appeared to have seen better days. She'd bet anything it was Charlie's. He didn't appear to value taking care of his things.

Celine leaned back and sagged in the chair. She didn't want to think about what had just happened with Jayson. Heat pricked her skin and she dug her nails into her palms as she thought about the way he had blown her off. At the same time, her stomach bottomed and her cheeks warmed. Why had she put herself in that position to begin with? She'd made herself vulnerable to him, and she never should have.

She lifted the lid of the laptop and stared at a gamer screensaver. Crusader-something.

Maybe she could get a hold of Monty. He might know how to get her out of here since his ranch neighbored Jayson's. She hit enter and a login box popped up. Damn. There went that idea.

Yet, Charlie wasn't the brightest crayon in the box. She looked at the screen. *Crusader*. Would he be that dumb?

She typed in the word.

The screensaver vanished and she was in.

*Yep. That dumb.* She rolled her eyes, while at the same time her muscles relaxed with relief.

Celine leaned forward and studied the screen. First, Celine

wanted to let Meredith know she was doing fine. She hadn't been in the mood to talk with anyone on the phone—it hurt her head to talk too much—but a quick email would be all right.

She logged onto one of her web email accounts, composed a quick email to her friend, and promised to be in touch again. When she was finished, she logged out.

Next, she wanted to figure out how to make funds available when she couldn't get to a bank. Maybe she should see what was in her accounts now.

Wait, was her accounting software still hijacked by the ransomware? Could she even get into the programs? It had only been a short time since she'd told Monty to get the best protection he could for her accounts and her designs. Had he done that?

She brought up the Internet browser and typed in her company's remote access site. She let out a breath of relief when she logged into her company's accounting software.

Celine frowned as she examined the records. Her accounts, while still healthy, appeared to have considerably less in them since the last time she looked.

Twenty thousand had gone to the ransomware, according to Monty. But what were these other charges? She did a mental calculation. It appeared that her accounts had dropped by at least fifty thousand since the last time she'd looked, maybe a week ago.

Her heart thudded. One of three things could be responsible —the accounting was wrong; or she'd had some big unexpected expenses, like the ransomware attack; or maybe this time the virus had screwed up her books.

A fourth possibility existed that she didn't want to even consider—was someone in her company stealing from her?

She signed out of the remote access and went to her bank website, then logged in.

The summary of her accounts came up. Her stomach dropped to her toes this time, and her heart beat faster.

*Something must be wrong.* Her business accounts were close to a hundred thousand less than the last time she had looked. That was close to double the amount of funds that appeared to be missing in her business accounts. It didn't make sense. As her CFO, Monty always did such a good job of keeping the accounting team on track and the accounts balanced.

What the hell happened? Did it have anything to do with the computer attack and her accounts having been held hostage?

She forced herself to breathe calmly. Monty could explain this. Everything was fine.

If only she had her phone, she could call him.

She stared at Charlie's computer screen. She didn't see an app for Skype. Where did he get his email? She looked at the row of icons at the bottom of the screen. One of these had to be for email.

A chat window at the lower right hand corner of the screen caught her attention. Monty had that instant messenger application—she'd chatted with him many times before with the same app. She could reach him that way, and it would be a lot faster than email.

She could sign out of his account and sign into her own, but it would be easier just to send Monty a message from here.

Tension in her body eased a little more as she clicked on the chat window. There had to be a rational reason for the difference in her accounts. Bills that hadn't been paid until now—something.

She went through the list of contacts until she reached Monty's name.

"Yes," she muttered aloud and selected the icon with his picture on it.

The keys made a click clack sound as she typed. *Monty, are you there?*

The cursor blinked a moment as she waited for his response.

*What do you want, Charlie?* popped up on the screen. *I'm in the middle of something.*

*This is Celine. My laptop is missing and I'm in your trailer on Charlie's laptop.*

For a long moment, nothing.

*Then, Celine, thank God you're safe. Jayson told me what happened. How are you?*

*Fine. Stuck here since the road is out. Looks like a crater over there.*

*In the same boat,* he typed.

*I need to talk with you. It's important.*

*What can I help you with?*

She took a deep breath then told him the news. *My company accounts and my bank accounts aren't even close to matching. What is going on?*

A long pause.

*I hope to the heavens that the hackers didn't attack again and just flat out take the cash,* he finally said.

*Did you get the software to protect the company from that?*

*Yes.*

That was it. *Yes.*

*Then what happened?* she asked.

*I'll look into it and get right back to you.*

Celine hurried to respond. *Is it possible for me to get to your ranch? I want to work on this with you.* She waited for him to reply.

A moment later, *If it's not out, there is a trail you can take.*

*Can I stay at your house? Sick of this place.*

Another long pause. Was there something wrong with the connection? Maybe it was taking longer than normal for her messages to reach him, too.

*Of course. I can meet you at the trail.*

She breathed out a long sigh as she spoke aloud. *How do I get there?*

He typed in directions that sounded easy enough.

*When?* popped into her box.

*As soon as possible.*

*That is for the best,* he answered.

The best for what?

He could probably use her help.

Celine peeked through the curtains of the trailer window. It was getting darker and stormier looking.

*She sighed and went back to the chat window. Looks like tomorrow will be better. A storm is likely hitting soon.*

*Message me in the morning when you're ready, he responded. In the meantime, I'll check out everything in detail.*

*Thanks, Monty. You're the best.*

No response.

She lowered the lid of the laptop and put it back into sleep mode.

A knock at the trailer door startled her. *Who—*

Of course, it had to be Jayson. No one else was around.

She debated on whether or not to even answer.

"I know you're in there." He knocked again. "I'm coming in one way or another, Celine. We need to talk."

How did he even know she was there?"

Oh, duh. She'd left the rubber boots outside the door.

"You're pissed at me and with good reason." She couldn't read his tone as he spoke. "But I'm not going to stand out here and yell about it through the door."

Celine pushed herself to her feet and practically stomped to the door. "Go away."

"Not on your life."

"Then someone else's life." She scowled. "Just leave."

"Nope."

Heat flushed her skin and she jerked the door open. "I said go—"

He stepped into the trailer, forcing her backward with his sheer presence

She planted her feet, raised her chin, and fisted her hands at her sides.

In a movement too fast for her to stop, he caught her in his arms and brought his mouth down hard on hers.

Celine's mind spun with the thrill of his intoxicating kiss. She felt drunk with it, drunk with him.

She didn't hesitate to respond. She'd wanted him since she first met him, in this very trailer.

His western hat was in the way and she pushed it off, then heard the thump of it on the carpeted trailer floor. She slid her hands down his chest then pulled his T-shirt out of his jeans and ran her palms up the hard planes of his abs to his marvelous pecs. He felt even better than she'd imagined.

His hands roamed her back, but he didn't go any farther than that. She'd never been kissed like this in her life.

Jayson drew back. Her breathing came hard and fast and she saw his did, too.

He met her forehead with his. They stood for a long moment as she waited for him to say something, to do something.

When he raised his head, she looked into his eyes. They were filled with passion and desire. Yet, at the same time something else was there, too. Regrets?

"I want you, Celine." His voice came out rough. "But we have to talk."

"Okay." She cleared her throat. "Here?"

He looked at their surroundings, Charlie's mess all around them. He sighed and stepped back from her before scooping up his western hat. "It's as good a place as any."

"The place is a disaster right now, but the couch is comfortable." Celine took Jayson's hand and led him to the leather couch across from the computer desk where she'd been working.

His hand felt so good in hers. Warm and callused, it was the hand of a man who performed hard work.

They sank onto the couch, but Jayson shifted, sat on the edge, and angled to meet her gaze.

"What do you need to talk about?" she asked softly.

He blew out his breath and shook his head. "I'm afraid, Celine."

She cocked her head. "Afraid of what?"

"Myself," he said. "What I'm capable of."

"I don't understand," she said slowly. "Can you please explain?"

He braced his forearms on his thighs and looked at his hands before meeting her gaze.

He hesitated a little longer, then said, "When I was twenty-two, I almost killed a man I'd considered my friend."

A chill rolled through Celine during the heavy silence. Her words to him earlier, about not having murdered someone in cold blood flashed through her mind. Had he nearly done exactly that? "How? A brawl of some kind?"

Jayson met her gaze. "I caught him trying to rape a girl we'd grown up with." Jayson shook his head. "I lost it. I saw red and I could have killed him if I hadn't found the strength to stop." His throat worked as he swallowed. "I put him in the hospital."

Celine felt a weight press down on her as she thought about what Jayson had said. The guilt he carried from what had happened must have been tremendous.

"You saved the girl," Celine said.

"Yeah." Jayson dragged his hand down his face. "I don't regret that. But I took it too far."

"You were twenty-two." Celine leaned forward. "You made a mistake. Everyone makes mistakes."

He eyed her steadily. "Not everyone nearly kills someone."

She needed to make him see things differently. "That was something like sixteen years ago?"

He gave a brief nod.

"Have you ever lost control like that again?"

"No." He studied her as she held his gaze. "But it's in me. If I did it once, I'm capable of doing it again."

She grasped one of his hands in hers and squeezed it. "I did things when I was young that I'm not proud of. But I've changed. I've learned from those mistakes and I won't repeat them."

"Have you forgiven yourself?" He gripped her hand in return. "For the guilt you've carried all these years?"

She smiled faintly. "I hadn't until that day in the barn when I spent time with you and the horses. I carried that weight for all these years, but you and Shiloh and Starlight made me realize that my horse, Sky, wouldn't have wanted me to carry this weight. She was as human to me as anyone. I shared everything with her. She might have been a horse, but I think she was actually an angel."

A slight smile curved Jayson's lips. "I think you just might be right. My dad always said the same thing about dogs. They were sent to us from Heaven." He flashed a grin. "Cats though, my dad thinks they're from down south."

Celine smiled. "Where's Thor? He's a good example. He helped save my life."

"Yes, he did." Jayson shifted on the couch. "He's back at the house. I told him to hold down the fort."

She put her other hand over their clasped ones. "Back to this guilt you are holding onto. What are you going to do about it?"

He had a faraway look in his eyes and appeared to be turning it over and over in his mind. He said nothing.

Celine tried again to break into his thoughts. "How is the girl?"

Jayson's gaze came back into focus. "She's doing well. Married, four kids, two dogs, and a pet squirrel that hangs out in the backyard."

Celine laughed before letting her tone become more serious. "Then you need to think about that. Being raped could have made her emotionally unavailable. It happens. You might even have saved her life."

Jayson blew out his breath and looked at their joined hands

before meeting her gaze again. "I'm going to have to think on this."

"I understand." She smiled gently. "We have both been living with guilt almost too great to bear. It's time to let go."

He untangled his fingers from hers and stood. "Come back to the house with me and I'll make dinner. Then how about a movie?"

"Okay." She got to her feet. "That sounds nice."

He rested his palms on her shoulders. "I'm sorry about earlier."

"You have nothing to be sorry about." She leaned forward and brushed her lips over his. "I get it."

He gave her a soft kiss in return before leading her out of Monty's trailer.

## CHAPTER 10

"You make fantastic tacos." Celine settled on the loveseat in the living room and tucked her feet beneath her. Their "talk" yesterday seemed like it happened ages ago. "The best meal of the last week or so of our entrapment. As a matter of fact, the best tacos anywhere, in my book."

Jayson grinned and stretched out on the couch. "I'll take that as a compliment."

"You should." She leaned back against the cushions as Thor hopped onto the cushion beside her. "I've been in some great Mexican restaurants, and theirs don't come close."

"That's because the best ones aren't big fancy places. The restaurants that can't be beat are the little dives." Jayson propped himself on his elbow. "Once we get out of here, I'll take you to a terrific place, a hole-in-the-wall in Prescott."

"Perfect." She sighed and rested her hand on Thor's head. She rubbed him behind his ears and he made a pleased groaning sound. "Do you have a movie in mind for tonight?" They'd watched several of his older favorites on DVD over the past few nights since they'd had problems with reception and his online video account.

"Let's see if I can log on and look for something different." He used the remote to turn on his TV and select his account.

In moments, he pulled up a list of available movies. It would be nice to watch something current as opposed to the older movies he had on DVD. Not that she hadn't enjoyed them. They went through the list until they both agreed on an action drama about a woman searching for her husband who had mysteriously vanished.

Even though she and Jayson weren't sitting next to each other, Celine felt as if they were. A connection tethered them, like nothing she could ever have imagined. It made it difficult to focus on the movie. She wanted to be closer to him, to feel his body against hers as they watched the movie together. They were in the same room, but not close enough.

The day that had passed since they'd had the talk in Monty's trailer had been thick with tension, the sexual kind. Jayson had seemed the same as ever, but things had changed. Celine just didn't know which way they would lean.

Halfway through the movie, their gazes met and held. It was like it was just the two of them and nothing else in the room.

Jayson paused the movie and looked at her again. "You're not watching."

The corner of her mouth quirked. "Neither are you."

He gave a sexy half-smile. "Maybe we both have other things on our minds."

"Maybe you're right." She wrapped her arms around her knees. "You first."

He got up from his seat and took the few steps to reach the loveseat, then snapped his fingers and Thor jumped down. Jayson settled onto the cushion beside her.

His nearness was electric. She had to hold herself back from moving closer, sliding onto his lap, and kissing him. He clearly wanted her—she could see it in his eyes. But he didn't make a move and he didn't say anything.

She held her arms more tightly around her knees, bringing them closer to her chest, as if to protect her from what he might say. What if he told her they needed to keep their distance and not consider any kind of physical relationship?

Was that all she wanted—something physical?

*No.* She wanted more from Jayson. Maybe more than he was willing to give. Or more than he *could* give.

"Have you thought about what we talked about?" she asked.

"Almost nothing but," he said slowly. "I spent a good deal of my time considering what you said, and the rest thinking about you."

She held her breath and let it out slowly. "And the verdict?"

Jayson moved closer to her. She felt alive with his nearness, the electric connection sizzling and vibrant. She breathed in his scent and the warmth of his body radiated out to her.

Slowly, he brushed hair from her eyes. The strands slid across her cheek in a silky trail. She shivered, the contact causing all thought to vanish for that moment.

He cupped her cheeks in his palms and smiled.

She couldn't breathe. His mouth hovered over hers, his breath warm over her lips.

"You're right," he murmured. "Everything you said. I'm not the same young man."

She slid her fingers into his hair and pulled him down to meet her.

His kiss was long, making up for every moment that had been between them since they had met.

Every lonely moment that she hadn't been in his arms.

And now—there was no place on earth she wanted to be but right here in Jayson's arms.

He shifted her so that she straddled his hips. She drew back and looked down at him. A smile touched her lips. "You're a good man, Jayson McBride."

"And you're one hell of a woman."

He cupped the back of her head, drawing her down again until their lips met. His kiss was hungry, urgent now, and she threw herself into it with wicked abandon.

She needed him more than she had ever needed a man—or anyone else—in her life. He had become the very air she needed to breathe.

He groaned before holding her tightly to him and standing in one powerful movement. She smiled at the sense of urgency and desire he radiated as he carried her toward his bedroom.

She clung to him, her arms around his neck as she slid her lips along his cheekbone to his ear and nipped at his lobe as he strode faster.

She squirmed in his arms. He couldn't get there fast enough.

When he reached his room, he didn't bother to close the door behind him. He set her on the edge of the bed. She dragged her palms down his chest as he rose, and her fingers conveniently found his belt buckle in front of her face as he stood.

"No, you don't." He spoke with such a low timber to his voice that she shivered from the way it permeated her being and settled in her belly. It battled the butterflies dancing there, fighting to see which could make her more excited and nervous.

The combination lit her even more, and her desire threatened to combust within.

"Let me." It sounded like a demand when she said the words and reached for his belt. Maybe it was.

He shook his head. "No, honey. I'm in charge of this rodeo."

She grinned. "Rodeo?"

"Yes, ma'am." He gave a slow, exaggerated drawl. "Now, just hold your horses, pretty lady."

She giggled and he pushed her back onto the bed. He stripped off her socks then ran his fingers along the soles of her feet.

"That tickles." She tried to pull away, but he only tickled her more.

Caught between giggles and desire, she squirmed. She breathed a sigh of relief and disappointment when he stopped.

But considering he was toeing off his boots and stripping off his socks, she was doing just fine.

As soon as he'd gotten rid of his boots, he reached for her again. He unbuttoned the snug worn jeans and unzipped them before tugging them over her hips, leaving her naked from the waist down. She grew wetter between her thighs at being bared to him.

"Nothing on underneath." He grinned.

She laughed and tried to wriggle away from him. "That's what happens when your car is at the bottom of an arroyo with all your clothes in it."

"I'll keep that in mind for the future." He slid his hands up her legs. "Your skin is so damned soft."

He grasped her hips in his palms. Even with her height, she felt small, almost petite with him.

She shivered as he eased up and braced his knee between her thighs, close to her center. He pushed up the T-shirt he'd given her to wear, then easily pulled it over her head and tossed it aside.

"Beautiful." He stroked her skin, just above her breasts. His fingers were callused from hard outdoor work. She liked the feel of the roughness against her soft skin.

"Your turn." She tugged his T-shirt up, and he helped her pull it over his head before he dropped it to the floor.

"Wow." She let her gaze drift from his broad shoulders, down his torso to his jeans. The top button was undone. "That's so sexy." Her voice was breathy as she spoke.

She sat up on the bed and grasped his zipper pull and tugged it down. No sign of underwear, just a glimpse of hair what was so close to the prize. "So, you've gone commando, too."

"Wouldn't want you to feel alone," he said with a grin.

"With you I could never be alone." She wasn't sure why she said it aloud, but it was true. With him she would never feel alone in the world like she normally did. She'd had a couple of close friends in her life and had only dated a handful of men. But Jayson was more than any of that. More than a friend. More than a lover.

He was real. Solid. Stable. A rock. And she wanted him to be *her* rock.

*Whoa, Celine, she told herself. Too far, too fast. Enjoy the moment.*

She pushed down his jeans and he stepped out of them.

"You're magnificent." She raked her gaze from his legs to his cock. Big. Thick. "Every inch of you."

"You're going to make my head big." His teasing words make her look up. "Now why don't you come up here, baby."

She got to her feet and he brought her to him, wrapping her up in his strong arms, pressing her naked form to his. It felt so wonderful—his hard male body and strength were a perfect match to her softer body and gentle curves.

He skimmed his palms down to her ass, then ran them up her back to her shoulders. He explored her with his hands, as if he couldn't get enough of her.

She gripped his ass, feeling the hard strength of his buttocks in her palms as she explored him in return. She loved the feel of her breasts against his chest, their bodies molded together.

He caught her off guard when he swept her off her feet and plopped her down on the middle of the bed.

She laughed, her breath slightly knocked from her.

He came down on her so fast she thought he would squash her. But he braced his hands and knees to either side of her as he straddled her and looked down with a smile.

"You are absolutely gorgeous, inside and out." He stroked the side of her face as he said words she'd never heard before.

No one had ever said she was beautiful inside. People thought she was superficial and she wondered if maybe she was. But just maybe she wasn't.

His eyes met hers and their gazes held. She didn't know if she could ever get enough of the way he looked at her, the feel of his body pressed against hers.

Jayson lowered his head and brushed his lips over hers. Just a soft whisper of a kiss. He leaned back just enough to study her face. "I'm torn between wanting to be inside you so badly and taking the time you deserve." He gave a pained smile. "I can hardly control myself."

"Don't then." She wiggled beneath him as his cock pressed against her belly. It seemed to grow bigger just from her movements. "Take me."

He shook his head. "Not like that. You do deserve slow lovemaking. I want to worship every bit of you, Celine. Every part of who you are."

Her heart squeezed and she raised her head off the mattress. "Then kiss me."

Jayson lowered his head and took her mouth in a long, sensual kiss. Celine sighed into his mouth. Her mind spun with the kiss, her whole world tipping from the way he claimed her with his mouth and body.

He dragged his lips from hers, kissing a path along her jaw to her ear. He nipped at her earlobe, like she'd done to him, only his bite was a little rougher than hers had been.

It was so erotic. Everything he did was erotic...so sensual he took her places she'd never dreamed existed.

He slid his lips down the column of her neck to the sensitive skin at the hollow of her throat. He eased down her body, kissing her skin in a reverent way, as if worshiping every bit of her.

She wanted him, needed him. The way he made her feel, the way he set her on fire while teasing and filling her senses...she reveled in it and she didn't want him to hurry. She wanted to live and enjoy every moment.

He moved his lips up the curve of her breast and she shivered with anticipation before he sucked her nipple into his warm mouth. She gasped, arching her back without thinking about it. She begged for more without finding the words to say what she wanted.

She grew wetter between her thighs, need, desire, and pleasure winding throughout her. He sucked her nipple while stroking the opposite nipple and drawing it into an even tighter bud. He eased his lips down the curve of her breast, taking his time before he found her other nipple with his mouth.

She could never get enough of this, never get enough of his mouth, his hands, his mind. Never get enough of *him*.

He teased and tantalized her with his tongue and mouth. She whimpered needing *more*. His attention to her breasts was incredible. Could she climax from the exquisite sensations he gave her while sucking her nipples?

Higher and higher. She was rising like on a swell in the ocean. One that grew larger and higher, about to sweep her away—

He moved his mouth away from her breasts and she let out a cry of frustration.

"Your body is amazing," he murmured. "So responsive to my touch."

"How could I not be?" Tears of frustration and desire wet the corners of her eyes. "You're driving me crazy."

She looked up at him and he gave her a sexy grin. "That's the idea."

"You're evil." She shifted her hips as he neared her bellybutton. "You—"

He dipped his tongue inside and electricity shot from her navel to her clit as if a livewire connected them. She nearly launched off the bed from the sensation. She'd never felt anything like it before. And he hadn't even touched her clit yet.

He chuckled and she threw a pillow at his head. He flashed a grin at her as the pillow toppled onto the floor.

Jayson eased his big body between her thighs, pressing them apart, opening her wide to his view. He blew on her clit and she nearly came unglued.

The frustrating man wasn't even touching her clit, but the slightest hint of even a whisper was going to send her flying—

He moved his lips away from her folds to kiss the inside of her thigh.

*"Jayson."* The cry vibrated through her. "I don't want it slow anymore. I have to have you inside me."

Another low laugh. Another pillow hit him in the head.

"Good arm," he said even as he worked his way down to the inside of her knee and kissed the sensitive skin there.

"Did you take training on how to drive a woman crazy?" She had another two pillows she could launch at him. "You are about to drive me out of my freaking mind."

"Good," he said with a grin and she grabbed another pillow.

He kissed the inside of her ankle and she sighed with pleasure. She never would have guessed it would feel so good to be kissed there or that it would be so sensitive.

The maddening man kissed the inside of her other ankle then slid his lips up to the inside of her knee.

"It's official." Her breathing had grown ragged. "You have completely driven me out of my mind."

"There's more where that came from," he murmured as he reached the crease between her thigh and where she needed him most right this minute.

His tongue darted out and she squirmed, twisting in his hold on her hips, wanting his mouth where it counted most right now.

"Is there something you need?" His warm breath feathered her shaved mound. "Tell me."

Celine groaned and clutched the pillow to her chest. "Shut up and lick my clit. I need your mouth on me."

"Shut up?" he said. "Is that how you ask for something you want?"

She shifted the pillow to the side and looked at him again. "Please, Jayson. *Please.*"

Without so much as a warning, he buried his face against her.

She shrieked with surprise and pleasure that shot off the charts. One more lick and she was gone.

The climax crashed into her, sending her reeling, her mind flying. Powerful sensations took her away and she rode them.

It was the longest, most intense, most powerful orgasm she'd ever had, and it didn't want to let her go.

It went on and on, then a second hit her and a third.

Jayson hadn't stopped. She had been so wrapped up in the orgasm or three that she'd just felt, hadn't thought.

"Stop, stop, stop," she said as she tried to wriggle out of his grasp. "Can't handle—please, no more."

She met his gaze as she fought to control her breathing. He watched her as he slid two fingers inside her core. Another spasm hit her and she threw the third pillow at him as she bucked.

He snorted out another laugh and crawled up her body so that he was over her again, his hands propped to either side of her shoulders, and his knees straddling her hips.

His eyes had gone a shade darker. "Ready for me inside you?"

She shook her head. "Not now."

He raised his brows. "Oh?"

She gave a satisfied grin. "Your turn."

Jayson gave her a cocky grin. "I have control, honey."

She reached between them and wrapped her hand around his cock and squeezed. "Really? Should I go for your balls, too?"

He winced, then his expression melted into one of both pain and pleasure. "You win," his voice sounded rough.

"I know." She kept her grip on his erection. "Roll onto your back."

He grimaced. "Promise you'll give it back when you're done with it."

She moved with him. "You may not want me to."

"True." He settled on his back and she knelt between his thighs. She didn't let go. With her opposite hand, she cupped his balls and lightly squeezed.

Jayson winced again. "Careful with the family jewels. I'd like to have kids one day."

Celine hesitated. Kids? She'd never thought about him wanting to be a father one day.

She brushed the thought away and held his gaze. She trailed her fingers up and down his cock and over the head. He hissed out his pleasure. With slow, deliberate movements, she stroked his cock from the base to tip, brushing her thumb over the top and through the pre-come at the head.

"You're getting even." He captured her face in his hands. "I need you, baby."

She squeezed his cock and lightly did the same with his balls. Only enough to tell him she meant business.

"You win." He fell back, his head landing on the remaining pillow. "But this is one time I don't mind losing."

"Aren't you glad you lost that bet?" She lowered her mouth to his cock as she held his gaze. "We wouldn't be here if you hadn't."

He groaned. "Make that two times I'm good with losing."

"I'm glad to hear it," she said a moment before she slid her lips over his cock.

---

JAYSON'S whole body went limp as his woman slid her warm mouth down the length of his erection.

When had he started thinking of her as his woman? Didn't matter, because she was. He had never met a woman like Celine, had never felt any connection like he did with her.

He could barely think as her hot, wet mouth devoured him. She took him to the back of her throat and he thought he'd never be able to speak again. All he could do was grunt like a caveman wanting his woman.

*Now.* He heard the Neanderthal voice in his head. *Man want woman. Man want woman now.*

He was losing his mind. Every last bit of his sanity had pooled in his cock, and Celine had just finished stealing it. The ache there magnified, grew stronger, until he thought for sure he was going to light up like a Christmas tree on fire. One match and he would burst into flames.

Wouldn't take much.

How far could he let her go without rocketing over the edge into a full-blown orgasm?

No. He had to wait to be inside her. He wouldn't lose control like that.

She sucked hard, the suction of her mouth sending that thought straight out of his mind.

Abruptly she stopped.

The orgasm that had been building soared out the window. He looked at her from beneath his lowered eyelids. "I'm ready to take you," he said in a low growl.

She applied light pressure to his cock and balls with her hands. "I don't think so."

She wasn't hurting him, and he was confident she wouldn't—mostly. Still, the thought that she had that power over him made him wince again.

She stroked his cock in a slow, sensual movement, while keeping one hand on his balls. "Going to be a good boy now?"

His words came out in a grunt. "Yeah. But so help me, honey, if you don't hurry—"

She squeezed and he groaned and shut his damned mouth. He eyed her and she gave him a sexy, wanton grin. "You were saying?"

He gritted out, "You're enjoying this."

"You know I am." She slid down so that her lips were close to his balls. "Every second of it."

She licked the length of him before sucking one of his balls into her mouth.

"Holy shit." He struggled not to writhe so he wouldn't cause himself pain. It felt so damned good, while at the same time keeping him right on the edge of pain. Just a hint, but enough to control him.

He met her gaze and she gave him a naughty look.

*Yeah, she's loving this.*

She took her time, drawing first one ball into her mouth, then the other and sucking lightly on each while stroking his cock.

Jayson was so damned close to begging when she released him. She nipped the inside of one thigh, sending a small but sharp burst of pain through him.

"You like to live dangerously," he said.

She grinned and nipped the inside of his other thigh. She rose and eased up his body until she straddled him. Her bare body was soft and sensual, her breasts firm and full. Her nipples were large and stood at attention as she smiled at him. Her thick, long dark hair slid forward over her shoulder. Her eyes looked darker now, smoky and mysterious.

Celine shifted so that her folds rubbed his erection. The silken glide of her over her his cock nearly had him crossing his eyes.

But she didn't have hold of the all-important package anymore.

He caught her by her waist and she shrieked with laughter as he spun her and twisted so that now he was on top of her. He pressed his erection into her belly as he pinned her wrists over her head.

"Now, who has control?" He gave her a satisfied grin as he looked down at her. "You're mine to do with what I want."

Still laughing, she tried to struggle, but he trapped her legs with his. Her body felt so good beneath his. Flesh to flesh, nothing between them.

He caught her gaze and refused to let it go. She stopped struggling, her laughter dying away. Her lips parted as he looked into the depths of her brown eyes. A tremor ran through him at the need and desire he saw there.

Jayson eased his hips between her thighs and seated himself there.

Her throat worked as he studied her. "What are you waiting for?" she murmured.

He grabbed protection from out of the nightstand drawer, shifted, and in moments was completely ready for her.

He wriggled between her thighs, sliding his sheathed cock through her slick folds.

Her eyes fluttered closed as she gasped.

"Open your eyes." He released her wrists and cupped her ass, bringing their bodies even closer together. Still holding her with one hand, he grasped his cock and pressed it to the entrance to her core.

"Ready for me, honey?" he said in what might have sounded like a controlled voice when he felt anything but.

"Yes." She spoke in a hoarse whisper, then louder. *"Yes,* Jayson." She shifted, trying to get impossibly closer to him. *"Please."*

He pushed in only slightly and she caught her breath, her eyes widening. He stretched her and filled her, and she took every bit of him.

He eased in and out, setting a slow pace. She wrapped her thighs around his hips and clenched him tight.

She started to close her eyes, but he let out a low, guttural sound. "Look. At. Me."

Her eyes widened as she met his gaze. Her face was flushed, a light sheen of perspiration over her skin. She caught her breath when he pressed in deeper, reaching farther inside her.

"Jayson." His name on her lips turned him to liquid. "Please."

He picked up his rhythm, moving faster inside her, pressing harder, deeper.

The flush in her cheeks deepened. He couldn't take his eyes off her as she climaxed and cried out, *"Jayson!"*

The sound of his name on her lips and the feel of her core clamping down on his cock sent him spiraling forward. It threw him into an orgasm that shot him into another hemisphere.

Heat flushed through him, burning him up.

He shouted her name as her core spasmed around his cock.

Almost all strength left him and he barely kept from collapsing on top of her. He braced himself on his forearms, his face close to hers.

Their breaths mingled and he watched a droplet of perspiration roll down the side of her forehead.

"You are beautiful." Jayson spoke softly as he pushed damp hair from Celine's face. She looked radiant, a glow that came from within. "Simply beautiful."

She gave him a smile that lit up his world. She looped her arms around his neck. "You are one sexy cowboy, Jayson McBride."

He grinned and kissed her before he rolled onto his side, bringing her with him. She snuggled close and he breathed in the scent of her, the scent of them. It mingled together, intoxicating and soul-filling.

This whole thing—Celine, him, what he felt they had—was another world to him, one he wasn't used to, but one he *could* get used to.

He shifted so that she was even more secure in his arms. He kept her wrapped in his embrace, not planning on letting her go.

## CHAPTER 11

The bitch had better give him her passwords for her personal accounts right away, or he would start with shooting her in the leg. Once he got what he wanted, *then* he'd kill her, just not with his gun if he could help it.

He'd been worried she would leave now that the county had brought out equipment that made the arroyo passable again at his property and Jayson's. But it was working out just fine. He could do anything he wanted to her since the wash was passable and he could leave.

Monty looked up the fork in the trail that went higher into the mountains. He had other plans for getting rid of her. She'd never be able to tell anyone what he'd done.

His handgun pressed against his spine as he waited at the trailhead for Celine. He'd tucked it into his belt. He'd never shot anyone or anything before. But, this was all about MERF, and nothing else mattered.

*Nothing.*

He'd kill his own nephew if the spoiled shit got in his way.

Celine had decided she couldn't make it until today, and he'd wanted to go to McBride's ranch and drag her ass away from the place. He'd had to force himself to bide his time while putting more of his plans into effect.

Unfortunately, he'd had to bid that six hundred grand without the funds in his account. This was a cash deal, and he needed to be prepared. He prayed the other bidder would drop out rather than bid again. In the meantime, Monty would have to do all he could to pull the rest of the cash together.

He looked up at the sky. Growing dark again. The sun had been shining not fifteen minutes ago. He hated this place with a passion that made his stomach churn.

The sound of a branch snapping made him whip his head in the direction of the trail coming from McBride's ranch. Hopefully Celine hadn't brought him with her.

She rounded an outcropping of trees. The first thing he noticed was that she looked…radiant, different than he'd noticed during the entire time he'd known her. She wore a smile, like she was happy. Had he ever seen her *happy* in the past? Genuinely happy? Not that he could recall.

What could have changed her on a dime like that? Hell, it hadn't been that long since he'd seen her last. How could a woman like her suddenly change…?

A thought occurred to him out of the blue. No. It was jumping to conclusions, but still he wondered—had she been fucking McBride?

That was a leap—a giant one—but what else could have flipped her switch like that?

She waved and picked up her step. When she reached him, he had to look up thanks to her height. Another reason he hated her.

He tried for a natural smile, and hoped it didn't look forced. "You look good, Celine. After what you went through, I'd say you look fantastic."

"Thanks, Monty." Yeah, she glowed.

*Bitch.*

"Come on to the house." He inclined his head in that direction. "I've got some things to show you."

She fell into step beside him. He kept his gaze straight ahead, not wanting to look up to meet her eyes, not wanting to see the sappy look on her face. And he certainly didn't want her to see her death in his expression.

"What's going on with my business accounts?" she asked as they walked.

He shrugged as his spine crawled. "I'll show you once we get to my house and we can get onto the computer."

"Fill me in, Monty." Frustration laced her words. Gone was the happy note to her voice. "My accounts have been bleeding for months now. Expenses here and there. So many of them."

His skin chilled as he glanced at her. "All documented and necessary expenses. You know that. You've seen the records."

She frowned, shaking her head slightly. "That's true, I have seen the documentation." She met his gaze. "I am trying to wrap my mind around how many expenses I've had in the last six months."

"Getting hit by ransomware was a biggie, not to mention purchasing the protection you need from it happening again." Panic crawled up Monty's throat but he forced it back down. It wasn't like she could do anything about it now. Not long and he wouldn't have to worry about her at all. "You'll see everything when we get to the house and I can show you the records."

Her frown deepened. "Okay," was all she said.

It took less than fifteen minutes to reach his place and it was with relief that they walked from the forest onto his property.

He swept his gaze over what had been his for the last year. He was about to lose the ranch due to the bank foreclosing on him—he hadn't been paying his mortgage because he didn't intend to be here past this month. He'd be in Belize, soaking up the clear air, the sun, and all the comforts his newly acquired wealth would give him. MERF would take care of him for the rest of his life.

They took the path down the trail that went to the back of the corral.

"Where is all your livestock?" Celine's voice knocked him out of his thoughts. Didn't you mention you have cattle and horses? I heard something about a prize bull."

Monty waved off her question, with a casual, "Horses in the barn, cattle off roaming somewhere."

"Oh." She sounded puzzled. "I don't hear anything."

True, his place was eerily quiet now that he'd sold off everything and didn't have any ranch hands around to do the work.

"It's like that sometimes." He guided her toward the backdoor so she wouldn't see the house mostly empty of furniture.

They walked in and she stuffed her hands into her back pockets as she looked around the Spartan kitchen. Here he didn't have much more than a coffee maker, toaster, countertop convection oven, and can opener. A lot of people kept their kitchens free of clutter, so he doubted she'd be suspicious.

Celine followed him through the kitchen, down the hall, and to his office. This room looked the most lived in because he needed furniture here, where he did all his work. When she walked in, she let her gaze drift around the room. She froze when she looked at her laptop and her designer tote on his desk.

He pulled his gun out of the back of his belt.

She whirled on him, fury in her expression. "What are you doing with—" Her gaze dropped to his hand.

His hand shook slightly, but he aimed his gun at her heart.

## CHAPTER 12

Celine stared in shock at the gun. Her heart nearly stopped, then thudded hard enough her chest hurt.

She swallowed. "It's been you, hasn't it." She made the statement, knowing it was true. "You've been stealing from me."

"You might be a bitch, but no one could call you stupid." Monty motioned with the gun in the direction of his desk. He brought out a handful of papers that she recognized—the pages with the child's and her mother's footprints.

"Sign these." He stuck the signature pages and a pen in her face.

She took them from him. She hadn't had a chance to review them on the plane or later since he'd stolen the bag.

"What are these?" she demanded.

"Listen, bitch." He pointed his gun at her head. "Shut up and sign."

She saw the viciousness in his gaze. She didn't have a choice, so she scribbled her name on the pages.

He snatched them from her and set the pages aside.

"Was there really a ransomware attack?" she asked, already knowing the answer.

He chuckled. "Damn, I'm good. You were forking money over to me left and right. Now if you'd just have given me control of your personal accounts, I'd be in Belize by now."

Celine didn't think she'd ever felt so stupid in all her life. "I trusted you with my company." Her words were cold and hard.

"Which is why your company is going to go bankrupt." He shrugged. "And if you don't cooperate, you won't be around to see the nothing that goes to that so-called dream project of yours. What was it? Some kind of horse ranch for kids?" he chuckled as he spoke.

He gestured toward her laptop with the gun. "Now log on to your laptop and go to your bank's site and bring up your personal accounts."

Celine slid into the seat in front of her computer. What choice did she have? Her money wasn't as important as her life.

Her next thought chilled her through. Did Monty plan to let her live once she'd given him access to her personal accounts?

She looked at him. "You're planning to kill me."

"Why would you say that?" He looked amused, but it was a fake expression. "I just want your money, not your life."

"I don't believe you." She set her jaw. "Why should I give you my money if you're going to kill me anyway?"

Monty pointed the gun at her thigh. "I'll shoot you one leg at a time, starting with that one. Why don't you try me?"

Celine shuddered. She had to think of some way out of this, and being shot wasn't going to help.

She lifted the laptop's cover and retro flying toasters screensaver came up. She made slow, deliberate movements, trying to stall as much as possible. The more she hurried, the closer she could be coming to her death.

Could she get ahold of Jayson? How?

She'd told him where she was going and that she'd be back well before dinner—she'd planned to make her favorite casserole.

Would he come looking for her when dinnertime came and went?

Yes, but it would probably be too late.

She pictured herself in a pool of blood and shuddered again.

"Hurry up." Monty perched on the edge of the desk. He held his gun in his lap and she wondered if she could go for it and turn the tables on him.

*Fantasy, she told herself. This isn't TV and I'm not some kind of kickass hero in a movie.*

She had no fighting skills, unless you counted grabbing a pair of Jimmy Choo ankle boots out from beneath another woman's nose and avoiding getting slugged.

But she could use her brains. She just had to figure out how.

Monty's voice lowered to a menacingly low level. "Stop screwing around, Celine. I'm losing my patience."

The desktop, with a runway photo of a model wearing a Celine Original, appeared as the screensaver vanished.

She clicked on the web browser and brought up her bank's login page. She glanced at Monty and the triumphant look in his eyes made her want to pick up the laptop and slam it against his head.

Now there was a thought.

But he had the gun.

Her fingers seemed to be tied in knots as she typed in her password. She fumbled and an error message popped up that she'd entered the wrong one.

She glanced at Monty, and when she did, something caught her eye on the wall beside him and her gaze riveted on a word written in script.

*MERF.*

Where had she heard that before? It was unusual enough that it stuck out in her mind. Wherever she'd heard it was so deep in her memory that she couldn't grasp it.

Hard, cold metal pressed against her temple. "I'm sick of this. Get me into your accounts."

Her hands trembled as she turned her attention back to the login page.

"What's MERF?" she asked as she entered the password.

"Monty's Early Retirement Funds." He laughed. "I named my horse Merf back when I raced against your dad."

Her attention swiveled to Monty and she stared at him. She knew she was supposed to be doing something, but all she could do was stare at him.

"You raced horses against my father?" she said slowly.

Monty shrugged. "It was a long time ago, but yeah, I did."

"Why didn't you tell me?" Nothing was sinking in right now.

Monty moved his face closer to hers. "Because I didn't want you to know that our business relationship is built on revenge."

"Revenge?" A sense of horror crept over her. Something wasn't right. Something beyond revenge.

He nodded. "That's right. Back when you were a spoiled little bitch instead of an all grown-up bitch."

It came back to her, as if painted in a neon sign. *"MERF."* Horror punched her like a fist into her gut. "That word was painted on the barn door the night the horses were poisoned."

Her mind spun with the implications. "Did you murder the horses?" She couldn't take her eyes off him. "Did you murder Sky?"

"How did you—" He glanced at the sign with *MERF* written across it. He shrugged again. "Your horse was collateral."

For a moment, all she could do was stare at Monty, yet what she saw was Sky, dead.

Raging heat engulfed Celine. She could barely see, much less think.

She grabbed the laptop and swung it at Monty as hard as she could. She slammed it into his head so hard he fell off his desk and landed on his back with a loud shout.

The gun barked at the same time pain burst in Celine's calf. She screamed and dropped the laptop. Her leg gave out on her and she fell to one knee.

Blood began to spread across the jeans covering her calf. The pain was unbelievable. She'd never felt anything like it.

"Bitch," Monty screeched as he picked up her laptop and flung it at her.

It hit her in her breasts, knocking her breath from her. She collapsed onto the floor, trying to breathe at the same time pain burned in her chest and her leg.

Monty grabbed her by her hair and dragged her back to the desk. Her vision blurred and she felt as if tossed from one bank of the arroyo to the other by the flash flood, trees and debris slamming into her.

He dragged her into the chair and shoved her so that her spine hit the back of the seat. Blood coursed down his face from a wound on the side of his forehead, an egg swelling on his temple. He tossed her now closed laptop onto the desk.

The gun shook in his trembling hand as he pointed it at her. "Put in the fucking password."

Stars continued to explode in her mind as she lifted the lid. The flying toaster screensaver came up.

She tried to collect her thoughts and drag them back into her mind.

*Monty killed Sky.*

*Monty killed Sky.*

She had to remember the password now. The bank account page came up on the password screen.

"Stop taking so fucking long." Monty hit her in the face with his fist and her mind spun. He grabbed a handful of her hair and jerked her head back so that he was so close she felt his hot breath over her face.

Blood slid down over his cheek from the cut the laptop had made when she'd swung it at him. Red was even in his teeth, which he bared as he shouted at her, "Get into your fucking accounts before I shoot your other leg."

He shoved his gun under her chin, hot metal boring into her skin. "Better yet in your hip or your shoulder. I'm told that hurts like fucking hell. So do it."

Her entire body shook from the adrenaline and fear pumping through her body. Monty moved his gun and dug the barrel into her hip. Her fingers trembled and she struggled even more to get the right password in.

"One more try," he said with a coldness she'd never heard in his voice.

She carefully typed in the bank password.

Her accounts came up. Unlike the business accounts, these numbers were exactly what she'd seen when she'd logged in the night in the hotel. The largest amount was the one her parents had set up for her that she hadn't used since college, when she'd needed the funds for tuition.

"Finally." He shoved her to the floor.

She cried out as she hit the wood flooring, hard. She stared at her soaked pant leg. Blood continued to spread. She looked at her sock feet, the left one now red from the blood sliding down her leg.

She looked up and saw Monty's gleeful eyes. Her stomach pitched with the realization she'd likely soon be facing her own death.

Blood and sweat mingled on his face as he turned and looked at her with a maniacal expression. "Write down your passwords. I need them in case I get logged out."

She blinked at him as he handed her a pen and a sticky note. He was an idiot for not having her do this to begin with. She could write anything down and he wouldn't know any better.

"I watched you put in the password," he said in a deadly tone. "I will know if you write down the wrong one.

Her hand shook as she placed the sticky note on the floor and scribbled the screensaver password, and the one for her bank on the paper, only she switched two of the numbers. Three drops of blood fell on its surface before she handed it to him. She hadn't noticed her head was bleeding from him punching her, but now felt the sticky fluid rolling down the side of her face. He'd probably cut her with his ring.

Monty ignored the blood and set the note on the laptop. "Get up." He stood and kicked her when she didn't move.

His shoe connected with her calf and she screamed and wrapped her arms around her knee and rocked. Tears flooded her cheeks.

"Get up," he screeched as he raised his foot again.

Celine forced herself to scramble to her feet the best she could. Her head spun as she grasped the chair with one hand to balance herself. She almost crumpled again when she put the slightest weight on her wounded leg.

He looked at the blood on the floor. "Shit." He swung his gaze on her. "You weren't supposed to bleed. I had other plans." He clenched his fists. "Now I have to hurry and get you out of here."

Monty strode to her side. Her skin crawled as he wrapped his arm around her waist and pointed the gun at her side with his opposite hand.

"I'm going to help you," he said with deadly calm. "But I *will* shoot you if you try anything."

He would kill her anyway, she knew, but she was in too much pain to know what to do. She needed her survival instinct to kick in, but right now she could barely think straight.

Celine stumbled and bit her lip to keep from screaming.

Monty assisted her through the house, prodding her with threats.

Blood slid down her leg, her sock soaked with it.

"Now I'm going to have to clean up this damned mess," he snarled. "Blood everywhere. If I didn't have things to do, I'd make you clean it up."

She wondered if she should just drop to the floor and let him kill her. But she held onto a thread of hope. Maybe, just maybe Jayson would be out on his property and see them.

Monty urged her out of the house with him assisting her. He wouldn't even let her put on her boots. Tears continued to roll down her cheeks as they progressed to the foot of the trail that led to his property from the forest.

Rocks bit into her sock feet as she went up the trail with him. Monty threatened her if she made too much noise. As if the sound of a gunshot wouldn't. Still, she bit the inside of her cheek to keep from crying out.

"Now I have to cover the blood on the trail." He breathed hard from his weight and being so out of shape. He continually whined about one thing or another as they went. He jabbed the gun into her side. "All I need is a little more time to empty your bank accounts and transfer to MERF. I'll be free to do whatever I please."

"You're crazy if you think that will work." She held back whimpers and cries that tried to come out with every step she made. "They will figure out it was you."

He waved away her words. "I'll be long gone. I have a place in Belize I'm buying. Beautiful there," he went on. "This time of year the weather is perfect. I'll have people to care for me and do whatever I want them to do. I'll have solitude, and all the luxuries I desire."

"You're dreaming," she said then cried out when he jabbed the gun barrel into her ribs.

"Shut up," he ground out. "I swear I'll shoot you in the head if you don't shut up and move faster."

Celine's thoughts whirred, caught in the middle of pain, fear, and struggling to come up with something that could save her life.

They reached the fork at the trailhead, where she had met up with Monty. Could that have just been an hour ago? Two at most. She really didn't know, and it didn't matter. Did it?

Monty forced her to take the other trail at the fork. This one went up, higher onto the mountain.

Her breathing came faster. She felt lightheaded, and cold. So cold.

Not more than ten minutes passed as they went uphill, and Celine said, "I can't do this." She barely got out the words. "I-I'm so tired. I think I'm losing too much blood."

He stopped. "This is high up enough anyway."

Her limbs had turned to mush and he kept her propped up. Shivers wracked her body so hard her entire body shook with it. She couldn't save herself. Celine knew that now. She barely had the strength to stand. Even speaking was too difficult.

He pressed her away from the trail and they reached a rocky outcropping.

Monty push her to the edge, so that her heels rested on the very edge. He sounded almost amused when he said, "Goodbye, Celine."

He shoved her chest hard. She flailed as she tried to grab him.

Her hands caught only air as she tumbled over the edge.

JAYSON GLANCED at the clock and frowned before looking out the kitchen window once again. The sun poised just over the treetops to the west. Soon it would sink in the sky and darkness would settle over the mountain.

He'd missed her like hell today and had come home a little earlier just to be near her. But she hadn't been here when he arrived, and she still hadn't shown up.

Celine had said she would be back in the afternoon, early enough to fix one of her favorite dinners. She'd planned on having it ready by the time he got home from working up at the northern end of the property.

He sure as hell didn't care about dinner, but he did care about her. Evening wasn't that far away, and he didn't want her walking home alone in the dark and stumbling down the trail. She could fall and hurt herself. Maybe she already had.

He shook his head. Worrying wouldn't accomplish anything, and likely she was running late. She might have had more to accomplish with Monty than she'd realized.

The thought of Monty made Jayson's frown deepen. He'd never felt right about the man, and the misgivings seemed sharper now and not so vague.

Was Monty bad news? He was a hard man to read, but Jayson had felt like something was off with Monty after the night Jayson had lost the bet. He was usually a good judge of character, but in this case… Jayson had a feeling he'd been wrong to trust the man at all.

Could Monty have anything to do with the missing bag with Celine's laptop in it?

His brows narrowed. When she'd told him about the disparity in the business bank accounts and the company ledgers, he'd wondered, but Celine had insisted Monty was the last person who would do something like steal from her. If someone had embezzled from her, it had to be another employee.

Jayson shook his head as he mulled it over. Could Celine be wrong? Could it be that Monty was the one stealing from her company?

Could she be in danger from him?

She'd said Monty had sounded put out when she'd told him she was waiting a day to go to his place because another storm was due to come in. Yesterday's monsoon storm had been on the radar maps as it traveled in from the southern part of the state, sweeping up from Mexico, so it hadn't been a sudden storm that they were unprepared for. And it had been a hell of a storm.

Thor nosed Jayson's leg and he looked down. The dog trotted to the door and glanced back.

"You thinking what I'm thinking?" Jayson studied Thor. "We should meet her at the trailhead to make sure she gets home all right."

Thor barked twice.

"Then that's what we'll do." Jayson shook his head and grabbed his hat off the rack before opening the back door and screen. He stood on the doorstep and checked the sky.

He stared up. The sky had darkened from both an oncoming storm and the sun lowering in the sky. Wouldn't be long before they wouldn't be able to see well. He stepped back into the house and grabbed a flashlight that could damn near illuminate a stadium to use later if he needed it. He closed the door behind him.

He wanted to cover ground quickly, before it grew too dark. He headed to the barn and made quick work of saddling Starlight. He grabbed his shotgun and sheathed the gun in its leather scabbard that he'd attached on the side of the saddle. Then he rode her to the foot of the trail that let out onto his property.

Thor bounded ahead on the trail. Starlight's hooves sank into the soft, damp earth. The air smelled of oncoming rain.

Lightning illuminated the sky, and a short time later the roll of thunder followed. As they continued on, lightning flashed again, a rumble following much closer than the last one.

Jayson's lips settled into a grim line. He didn't like the idea of Celine being out here in the dark in the middle of a thunder storm.

They reached the trailhead. Thor checked out the ground and let out a low growl. He sniffed the ground toward Monty's ranch then kept his nose to the ground and headed in the trail in the opposite direction.

Thor cast a glance over his shoulder at Jayson, and seemed to say, "follow me." He took off and ran along the branch leading away from the trailhead, in the opposite direction of Monty's place. He bounded up the mountain and vanished around a bush and pine tree close together.

"Where the hell are you going?" Jayson whistled for Thor to come back as he guided Starlight to the trail to Monty's.

Thor barked and came back into view. He ran to Jayson, barked, then bolted back up the trail again.

Jayson glanced in the direction they should be going and cut his gaze back to Thor, who gave a sharp bark.

Could Thor know something Jayson didn't? He was a damned intelligent dog and he adored Celine. Jayson had never seen Thor take to anyone like he had taken to her.

Why would she go up that trail instead of the one leading to Jayson's ranch? Had she forgotten which way to go and took the wrong trail? It seemed unlikely, but she wasn't a ranch girl and wasn't familiar with this territory.

Jayson hesitated only a moment before he tugged slightly at the reins so that he and Starlight faced the direction Thor had headed. Jayson clicked his tongue and encouraged the horse to follow the Border Collie.

This trail was even less traveled than the other. Starlight picked her way through rubble and over downed branches.

Jayson watched Thor sniff the ground before he continued uphill.

What was Thor seeing that Jayson wasn't? He frowned and brought Starlight to a halt before he dismounted. He tracked the ground with his gaze and stopped when he saw a dark smear on a large leaf, and a splatter on another.

He touched the sticky fluid. He grabbed his flashlight from Starlight's saddlebag, then knelt and shone the light on the drop and the smear.

Black. He studied it on his fingers and saw it was actually dark red.

*Blood.*

His stomach knotted. Was he imagining it?

He looked closer at the smear that wasn't just on the one leaf. It went across three leaves, not just one. The leaves were smashed onto the ground, the smear in the shape of a partial footprint.

Was it Celine's?

In his gut, he knew it was.

Jayson's heart threatened to explode. He swung onto Starlight's back and called to Thor. "Take me to her, boy."

Thor darted up the path. Jayson and Starlight followed.

The sky had grown darker, but he could see far enough ahead to follow Thor.

Lightning flashed, brightening the way a moment at a time. The crash of thunder followed. Closer and closer yet.

Thor veered off the path. In moments, he started barking, the sound sharp in the forest stillness.

Heart thudding harder, Jayson dismounted and hurried after Thor. He flipped on the flashlight again and pointed it ahead so it illuminated the ground as he made his way through brush, grass, and pine trees.

Jayson came up behind the dog, who stood at the edge of an outcropping of rock. Thor stared over the edge of the outcropping, then at Jayson, and barked again.

His throat grew dry and his mind raced. Was she down there? Had she fallen to her death? Could she still be alive?

"Celine?" he called out. "Celine."

*Nothing.*

The forest remained silent.

Thor barked again. The dog bounded from one side of the outcropping to the other. He looked focused, intent on finding Celine.

Jayson lay on the rocks on his belly and peered over the edge, as far as he could go without falling over.

He caught a glimpse of a white object.

Thor's bark changed into one of menace and he snarled.
A fist of pain and fear slammed into his chest.
The white object wasn't an object at all.
It was a woman's arm…
The arm shifted and moved out of sight.

# CHAPTER 13

Celine moved her hand to her throbbing head. She blinked, trying to place where she was and what she was doing. Her head buzzed as she took inventory of her surroundings and the aches and pains in her body. Even her ears rang and she couldn't hear sounds other than the vibrations in her head.

Monty had shoved her off the side of the mountain.

For an instant she felt the same terror she'd experience when he'd pushed her, and her body trembled. She'd landed on a ledge maybe six feet down, rolled into a depression in the rock wall, and was mostly out of the rain that continued to fall.

Lightning lit up the forest like a strobe light, and thunder came only a second later.

She took inventory of her body and realized the leg she'd been shot in was numb. What did that mean?

The shelf she'd fallen on was strewn with rubble, and the gravel and rock bit into her body. To the right was a massive drop off. To the left was a trail that looked like something animals might use.

It was getting late, and it would be getting darker than it already was.

She needed to get to that trail and make her way back before it got dark. She didn't want to die out here. Bears and mountain lions likely called this terrain home.

More than anything, she wanted to be in Jayson's arms. She needed to *move.*

Celine bit back a cry when she rolled onto her belly, half-in and half-out of the rain. The leg she'd been shot in was numb, but the rest of her screamed with pain. She tried to crawl along the ledge, but her body wouldn't work properly and she had to drag herself across the wet rock with her forearms.

The trail lay just feet away now. She took deep breaths. With her leg shot, could she do more than haul herself from the shelf to the small trail? She'd sure as hell try.

Rain poured from the heavens, soaked her clothes, covered her skin. Her feet were bare—she'd lost Jayson's large socks she'd been wearing.

When she reached the trail, her stomach twisted. To one side, the trail dropped off, so sheer she couldn't see anything but treetops below. She forced herself to keep moving.

Celine gritted her teeth and worked her way up the muddy trail. She hadn't fallen far, but the fall had knocked her cold. She'd hurt like hell when she came back into consciousness.

A sound came to her ears now, muffled by the storm.

*Is that a dog barking?*

A shot rang out. Loud enough she heard it through the cotton in her head.

The dog let out a yelp and went quiet.

*Thor? Did someone shoot Thor?*

*No!*

"Guess I'll have to get rid of you now, McBride." Monty's shouted words came to her in between flashes of lightning and the boom of thunder. "Before that, you'll help me find out if Celine is still alive. When I looked, she'd landed on a rock shelf instead of going all the way down. I figured she might have survived, but it was a nasty fall."

"First, I'm going to kill you if Celine is dead." Jayson's raised voice was dangerously hard. "I'll kill you again for shooting my dog."

Monty laughed, sending a chill through Celine. She couldn't hear his next words.

Her thoughts spun, rapid-fire as she struggled to find the strength to move faster. Jayson was in danger and she needed to get to him. But how could she help him when she could barely crawl?

*I won't give up.*

This was Jayson. The man she had fallen in love with.

The revelation made her lightheaded.

Love at first sight? Maybe. *Yes.* She was a believer now.

She wouldn't go down without trying. If it was the last thing she did, she'd help him.

*I don't have much time.*

Celine got to her knees so she could crawl faster. Somehow, she managed not to scream with every movement she made. The men's voices carried down to her, but her head still throbbed and her hearing was off, so she couldn't understand them as she moved.

Maybe two minutes had passed since she'd heard Monty shoot Thor.

*Too long.*

Her head throbbed. Her body screamed. Higher, closer to the surface.

Monty shouted, his voice a loud snarl, "Figure out a way to get to her and bring her back up here."

Celine reached the surface and peeked over the edge. Starlight was three feet away.

Monty was a good ten feet from her and pointing a gun. She peered through the rain and followed the direction with her gaze.

Her body went cold when she saw he aimed it at Jayson, who stood in front of him.

She recognized the moment Jayson spotted her. He continued to look at Monty, but with a slight movement of his fingers, Jayson told her to get down.

"There's no way to get down to the ledge," Jayson said, no doubt not wanting Monty to see Celine behind him.

Celine ducked and searched for *something*. She didn't know what, or even what to do with it when she found it.

Maybe a stick to hit him with? A rock to throw at him?

Nothing, not even a piece of wood.

"Figure out a way," Monty snarled. "Or you're no good to me alive."

Her heart raced faster as she looked wildly around. Her gaze rested on Starlight—and the shotgun he'd carried with him.

*Shotgun.*

She had to get to that weapon.

Celine gritted her teeth as she rose behind Monty. Pain shot through her but she clamped her jaws tight.

Jayson gave the slightest bit of recognition that he saw her and he set his mouth in a grim line.

She slowly moved the three feet to Starlight. The storm masked any sounds she might have made, including her whimpers of pain. She reached for the shotgun and pulled it out of its sheath.

Jayson said to Monty. "Something like that could really kick you in the ass."

"What the hell are you talking about?" Monty sounded like Jayson had just thrown him a curveball. "Something like what?"

Celine aimed the shotgun at Monty—and shot his ass.

Jayson dropped flat to the ground. Monty's gun went off as he went down screaming. He landed on his side and hit his head on a rock.

Pain tore through Celine from the effort, but she looked at

Jayson to see him surge up then dive for Monty in one fluid movement. He knocked the gun from Monty's hand, sending it flying across the ground.

Monty screamed again as Jayson rolled him onto his backside.

Celine fought to find the strength to stay upright and to hold onto the shotgun. Too weak. The shotgun dropped to the muddy ground. She didn't have the strength to hold it up.

She spotted Thor as she fought to keep standing, and her heart lurched. He lay several feet away.

Hope shot through her in a cold spear as Thor shifted his position and tried to get up. Celine gritted her teeth and limped to the dog.

"My ass!" Monty shrieked over and over. "Someone shot me in the ass!"

Celine looked over her shoulder.

"I don't give a damn about your ass or you." Jayson straddled Monty and slammed his fist into the man's face. "What you did to her. You should die for it." A look of rage darkened Jayson's features and he raised his fist again.

*Don't.* Words shot through her mind. *Don't do it, Jayson.* If he seriously hurt or even killed Monty, Jayson might never forgive himself.

Jayson froze, as if someone held his fist back, restraining him.

Or rather, he restrained himself from beating the hell out of Monty—or worse.

Instead of killing the man, Jayson whistled to Starlight, who trotted closer, then Jayson got to his feet. Monty tried to move, but Jayson pressed his boot on Monty's chest. "Don't think about it. You're not going anywhere."

Starlight reached Jayson and he removed a rope from one of the horse's saddlebags. He rolled then shoved Monty onto his belly and hogtied the bastard so tightly he squealed. The seat of his pants was dark with blood and riddled with small holes.

Celine's knees gave out on her. Her body couldn't take it

anymore. She dropped to the wet ground and rolled onto her back, then stared up at the pines and blinked away rain. She turned her head to look at Thor.

The Border Collie struggled to his feet, clearly wanting to help. He limped slowly, favoring one shoulder. He went to Celine and lay down beside her. He licked her face and she wrapped her arms around his neck and buried her face in his wet fur.

Sticky blood from a shoulder wound covered her hands, but if it hurt him, he didn't flinch. He licked her cheek again, before resting his head on her chest.

Jayson left Monty in the hogtie and hurried to Celine's and Thor's sides.

Celine shivered so hard her body vibrated. She grew colder, her leg impossibly more numb.

"HOLD ON, BABY." Jayson's heart pounded a mile a minute as he pulled his T-shirt over his head and tore it into strips as he examined her leg and found a bullet hole in her jeans. His gut twisted. "You're shot in your leg. Anywhere else?"

She shook her head. Her face was paper-white. He used the T-shirt to bandage her leg and stem the flow of blood. So much. She'd lost so much.

At the same time he worked on Celine, he glanced at Thor. He couldn't work on them both at the same time, and Celine looked in worse shape. Thor looked in pain but alert as he licked Celine's cold cheek.

Thoughts flashed through Jayson's mind. He knew he couldn't live with himself if he beat Monty to death. He didn't want to be the kind of person to kill a defenseless man. But that didn't mean he'd feel bad if one of the mountain's Black bears got to him.

Jayson's hands were bloody despite the pouring rain. He hurried to grab his cellphone out of Starlight's saddlebag, then punched in 911.

Thankfully, they were in a place where he could get cell phone service.

He examined Thor's shoulder wound as he waited for his call to be answered. The line was filled with static.

In moments, with just a little prodding, Jayson discovered that the bullet had gone straight through the muscle on his leg, somehow missing his chest. Probably the angle Monty had shot him had gone through just right. It didn't look like he was losing much blood.

Emergency services answered Jayson's call and he arranged for medevac as he tied a strip of his shirt around Thor's leg.

The operator told him to stay on the line, but with the rain, the thunder, the situation, Jayson couldn't hold onto the phone and get Celine and Thor to safety.

Jayson had to make it to the pasture where the helicopter would land before Celine lost more blood. It was ten minutes by horseback

For the second time, Jayson found himself with Celine's life in his hands, and it scared him shitless.

No doubt about it, she had saved his own life when she'd shot Monty in the ass. And she'd done it when she was weak and battered.

He managed to get her into Starlight's saddle. Her grip on the pommel wasn't strong, and Jayson had to work to get Thor onto the saddle with her. She wrapped her arms around the dog and buried her face in his wet fur.

Jayson mounted the horse behind her and Thor. Damn it. He had to keep them both safely on the saddle.

Monty was still sobbing and whining. "Don't leave me here, McBride. It's dangerous."

Jayson looked over his shoulder at Monty. "Sheriff McBride will be here shortly. Just hope that Black bears and mountain lions don't get to you first."

With that, Jayson clicked to Starlight, and they took off.

Somehow the horse knew to go to the north pasture. Jayson kept one arm wrapped around Celine's waist while using his other to hold Starlight's reins. Celine kept a hold of Thor.

Ten minutes later they left the tree line and made it to the north pasture. His ranch hands had relocated the cattle to the west pasture, a couple of weeks ago, so that would not be an issue when the helicopter arrived.

Medevac made it a few minutes after Jayson and Celine.

From that point on, everything blurred, seeming to go fast, yet too damned slow.

The paramedics rushed Celine into the helicopter, but didn't allow Jayson or Thor to accompany her.

Jayson didn't wait for the helicopter to clear the tree line. He took Starlight at a gallop to the barn, with Thor in front of him on the saddle. He had to stop to open and close two gates to make it to the barn from the pastures. Every moment it took, was a moment too long to Jayson.

They reached the barn and he hurried to take Starlight's saddle off and put the horse in her stall.

Jayson made short work of getting to the house, stuffing a change of clothes into a duffel bag, and grabbing everything he needed.

Thank God, the arroyo had been cleared out yesterday afternoon, or Jayson might have had to take the horse on a roundabout route to get to a neighbor's home and borrow a vehicle.

Jayson climbed into his silver Ford truck, and Thor rode on the passenger seat. Jayson would take him to the vet and then go on to the hospital. He made his way off his property and hit the road to the vet.

At the vet's office, the techs and vet took Thor right away. Jayson couldn't force down the knot in his throat. After a quick examination, the vet affirmed that the bullet had gone through and didn't appear to have damaged anything. Thor would be fine and they would take care of him.

Jayson bolted out of the vet's office to his truck, and headed for the hospital.

When he arrived at the ER, he threw the truck into park and nearly bolted inside.

He strode up to Lissa McBride, one of his cousins, who manned the front desk. He worked to keep his fear in check, but tension radiated through his body.

"Lissa, I need to locate Celine Northland," Jayson said. "Where can I find her?"

"Hold your horses." Lissa's dark hair bounced around her face as she leaned forward and typed on her keyboard while looking at the screen. She glanced up at Jayson. "Celine is in surgery."

Even though he knew it wouldn't do any good, he said, "I need to see her."

Lissa pointed to the waiting room. "You'll just have to take a seat like everyone else, Mr. McBride."

Frustration tightened his muscles and he leaned in close. "I need to know how she is, Lissa."

"Considering she's not a McBride, I'm pretty sure you're not immediate family," Lissa said. She gave Jayson a meaningful look. "Unless you're engaged?"

"Yeah." Jayson pushed up his Stetson and speared his fingers through his hair. "I'm her fiancé. How is she?"

Lissa looked at her computer monitor again. "Congratulations on your engagement, Jayson," she said overly loud. "Your mama must be excited to be getting a daughter."

He waited for Lissa to check on Celine's progress. He nearly groaned—he'd have to call his mom. This engagement thing was going to tear through town like wildfire. But was that so bad? He'd already decided that she belonged to him.

"Celine is in critical condition." Lissa put her hand over Jayson's as the words tore through him. "I can't tell you more than that. Once she comes out of surgery, Dr. Burgess will be notified you're here and she will let you know the status."

Jayson blew out his breath. It wouldn't do any good to get worked up more than he already was. Everything would be fine. Celine needed him to stay strong.

"Thanks, Lissa." He turned to the nearly empty waiting room, but didn't take a seat. Instead, he paced from one end of the room to another.

His heart hadn't stopped thumping and he wasn't sure it would settle down until he knew she was all right.

His muscles were so tight he felt like his body might snap.

He paced. And paced.

How long was this going to take?

After a while, one of the sheriff's deputies and Sheriff Mike McBride came in to take Jayson's statement.

"Monty Tinsman has been admitted to the hospital," Mike said. "Seems he got shot in the ass with a shotgun."

Jayson nodded. "Tinsman had a gun on me and was about to shoot. Celine saved my life by what she did."

Mike nodded. "We arrested Tinsman, then had him admitted to the hospital and he's under guard."

Mike had to go out on a call a short time later, leaving Jayson alone with his thoughts again.

"Mr. McBride?"

Jayson's attention sliced across the room to the doctor, who wore blue scrubs.

She held out her hand. "I'm Dr. Burgess."

"Doctor." Jayson nodded and gripped her hand.

She squeezed his in return then withdrew. "Celine's in recovery now," Dr. Burgess said. "Things were a little rocky, but providing all goes well, she should be able to go home in a couple of days."

The wash of relief that went through Jayson nearly rendered him boneless. For the first time since he made it to the hospital, he wanted to collapse on one of the chairs and take deep breaths.

The doctor explained about the extent of Celine's blood loss and that they'd removed the bullet.

"She'll be taken to a private room, and you'll be able to see her," Dr. Burgess finished. "A nurse will take you back when Celine is settled."

"Thank you, Doctor." Jayson gripped her hand again. "Thank you."

She smiled and squeezed his hand in return. "Celine will be fine," Dr. Burgess said. "She's a strong woman." She smiled before she turned and left.

"You don't know the half of it," Jayson said below his breath and allowed himself a small smile.

CELINE's whole crew showed at the hospital. Rod had called Jayson not twenty minutes before, trying to track down Celine. When Jayson gave him the news, Rod had rounded up the bunch and now they filled the waiting room.

"Mr. McBride." Lissa called out over the conversations in the waiting room. "You can see your fiancée now."

Everyone went quiet. Could have heard a bee's knees shaking.

"Thanks, Lissa." Jayson tried not to show any emotion in front of Celine's crew.

"Fiancée?" Rod said as Jayson made his way past.

Jayson shrugged. "I work fast."

"I'll say." Rod grinned. "Congratulations."

"Thanks," Jayson said dryly as he left the room behind Lissa.

"You enjoyed that," Jayson said as he fell into step with her.

She flashed a grin. "You know I did. Paybacks for the mouse in my lunchbox."

"Really?" Jayson tried not to laugh. "That was some thirty years ago."

She stopped in front of a door to a private room that was

about six inches open. "Some things are better left until the perfect time arises."

Jayson shook his head then took off his Stetson and entered the room.

His throat tightened when he saw how white Celine's face was. The dark curls around her face emphasized the china-paleness.

"Fiancée, huh?" she said with a faint teasing smile.

He released a grin. "You said yes back on the mountain."

"I-I" She looked both startled and confused. A smile lit her features. "Ha ha."

"I wouldn't joke about a thing like that." He took the seat beside her bed and put his hand over hers. "Celine McBride has a nice sound to it."

She rolled her eyes. "Give it up, Jayson. I know I wasn't that far out of things. I would remember if you had proposed."

He shrugged. "I'm holding you to your promise."

She shifted on her pillows. "You're supposed to treat the patient delicately, don't you know that? Not torture her with threats of marriage."

Jayson grinned and chuckled. "Whatever it takes, honey."

She touched his knuckles. Her fingers were so cold, that he captured both her hands with his so he could warm them.

A nurse bustled in and went to the IV. "Time for your meds, Celine."

"Didn't you just give me some?" Celine asked.

"It's been longer than you think, I we want to keep you comfortable." The nurse was finished in a few moments. She turned to Jayson. "Five more minutes."

He nodded. "Yes'm."

The nurse left the room and Jayson's gaze returned to meet Celine's.

Her features had softened even more and he saw her body

relax dramatically. The pain med in her IV must really be kicking in now.

"Thank you." She searched his gaze, her beautiful eyes reading into him. "You saved my life not once, but twice."

"Don't forget you saved my life," Jayson said. "If it wasn't for you, Monty would have killed me."

"I don't know what I would have done if he'd killed you." Her throat worked as she held his gaze. "I was so afraid that he would." She hesitated. "I can't imagine a world without Jayson McBride."

His heart constricted. "What are you saying?"

Celine smiled. "If I'm making a mistake, we can just let it slide as I'm delirious."

He raised an eyebrow.

She squeezed his hand. "Will you marry me, Jayson McBride?"

You could have knocked him over with a strand of spaghetti.

He couldn't take his eyes from her beautiful face. Even in the midst of machines and IVs, hospital gown and tousled hair. She was gorgeous.

"I expected to be proposed to on one knee," he said.

She waved away his statement in a way that made her look as if she'd had too much to drink. "I'll make it official later. Dinner, flowers, down on one knee, ring—the whole nine yards."

"You *are* delirious," he said. "But that's all right. I'll take you up on your offer."

"I'll make an honest man of you, Jayson." Her eyes grew droopy. "I love you." Her body went lax. In moments, her breathing became deep and even as she slept.

He shook his head, not sure what to make of Celine's proposal. Had she been teasing?

Hell, he didn't care at this point. She already belonged to him. He'd snatch her up before she changed her mind. But he'd insist on the whole nine yards—just to tease her—then do it himself.

He leaned over and kissed her cheek. "I love you, Celine."

When he leaned back, her lips curved into a smile and she looked completely at peace.

# CHAPTER 14

Celine listened to the night sounds as she and Jayson sat on the pond's dirt bank in the east pasture. Gentle moonlight touched his features, making the hard lines of his face softer. Starlight and Shiloh whickered as they ate grass.

Thor rested nearby watching the night, ears perked, probably hearing things she and Jayson couldn't.

She'd been back from the hospital for a week now, and this was her first venture onto the ranch since she was shot. She had pleaded with Jayson, insisting she was fine enough to make this trip. He'd been acting like a mother hen, but at least he hadn't been smothering her.

"You're quiet." He touched her fingers with his. "That doesn't happen much with you."

"It's a beautiful night." She smiled and turned her hand so that their fingers linked. "I'm enjoying it."

Jayson looked at her bandaged thigh, her leg stretched out in front of her. "Does it hurt?"

Celine thought about lying, and instead shrugged. "It does, but not too bad."

His forehead wrinkled. "Maybe we should get you back to the house."

"Jayson." She shook her head. "I've never been so mothered in all my life."

He spoke in a low voice. "Maybe it's time you were."

She looked away from him and watched the water in the pond ripple in the light breeze. "This place…" She shook her head. "I've never felt so full of life before."

The silence between them was comfortable. He didn't have to answer verbally, because she felt his response in the way he lightly squeezed her hand.

Somehow this place, this land, had captured her heart and soul in a way she had never expected.

She didn't want to go back to the clash and clang of New York City. The harshness, the brashness. This land had changed her. She wasn't the same woman she'd been when she'd arrived and his and her worlds collided.

But that collision had softened her. The land had softened her. She knew she could never go back.

She was a different woman now. A woman in love with the man who held her hand.

Her face warmed as she thought about the day in the hospital when she'd proposed to Jayson in her painkiller-induced haze. He hadn't said a word about it since.

Had she really proposed, or had it been her imagination?

"I must have damaged my head more than I realized," she said to herself, then realized she'd said it too loud when Jayson looked at her.

He raised a brow. "Oh?"

She shook her head and went for a smile. "You know what I mean."

"Maybe I do." He shrugged. "I'm wondering if you might be referring to a certain thing you said when you were in the hospital."

Now her face was *really* warm. "Oh?" Her turn to sound ambiguous.

The moonlight shone bright enough that she saw the corner of his mouth curve. "Something about 'the whole nine yards.'"

"I have no idea what you're talking about." She raised her chin. "Are you referring to a football game or something?"

He laughed. "I don't think for a second you don't remember."

She refused to look at him. "Whatever it was, I must have been delirious."

Jayson caught her chin in his hand and turned her face so that he could look into her eyes. "I want that whole nine yards, Celine."

In that moment, she couldn't breathe. What was he saying?

He released her chin. "And since you won't do it, I will."

Tingles raced through her body. Was he—?

Jayson shifted and moved so that he was on one knee, facing her. He held out a small box he must have pulled from his pocket.

Her heart raced and she didn't think she could breathe.

"We've known each other a short time, Celine." He smiled. "But my heart knows you. And your heart knows me."

She swallowed.

Jayson flashed a wicked grin. "And there's always the fact, you proposed first."

Heat flushed over her again, but this time it was different.

"I love you like crazy." He held her gaze as a shiver trailed her spine. "I want to spend the rest of my life with you." He opened the box, revealing a marquise diamond solitaire that winked at her in the moonlight. "Celine Northland, will you marry me?"

"I-I." She swallowed again.

"You already proposed to me." His smile broadened. "This is simply a formality."

She couldn't help but laugh. "In that case, the answer is yes. Yes, I will marry you, Jayson McBride." She couldn't help but smile even more. "It just so happens I love you an insane amount, too."

He slid onto the bank beside her, and took her left hand and slipped the ring onto her finger. "A little loose, but we'll get it adjusted."

She smiled. "It's perfect."

He lowered his mouth and kissed her silly. She knew he would have swept her into his arms if he wasn't concerned about hurting her, so she pulled him closer and ignored every ache and pain. They faded away, and all she could think about was his kiss, his scent, his heat…and her incredible love for this man who had changed her world forever.

JAYSON AND CELINE REACHED HIS PARENTS' home and they paused on the porch steps. Laughter and chatter carried through the open window. Sounded as if the whole clan might be on the other side of that door.

He looked down and smiled at his woman and pressed his fingers to her waist. She was beautiful as hell, intelligent, and everything he'd ever wanted in a mate. And she belonged to him.

"Ready for a McBride Fourth of July cookout?" The smell of mesquite wood burning in a barbeque grill carried on the breeze.

"I don't know." Celine held her hand to her belly, as if to settle the butterflies. "I'm so nervous."

He slid his hand around her waist and drew her close before kissing the top of her head and breathing in the soft floral scent of her hair. "You'll like my family. They're good people."

She met his gaze. "I'm not concerned about that. If they're related to you, I know they're going to be awesome in-laws. I'm worried what they'll think of me."

"Hey." He caught her chin, her skin soft beneath his fingers. "I love you. They will love you. Beginning of story."

She laughed. "Beginning of story?"

"Ours has just begun." He brushed his lips over hers, feeling a tenderness unlike anything he could imagine. "They will love you throughout our story. Just remember that."

Tears welled in her eyes, making them sparkle in the porch light. "I hope so."

"None of that." He kissed her again. "You deserve a family who will love you and believe me, you'll get more than enough with the McBride bunch."

He continued to hold her around her waist as he rapped on the door with his knuckles.

"That must be Jayson." His mother's voice. "And his bride to be."

"How does she know?" Celine cut her gaze to Jayson's. "You just proposed last night."

"We both proposed." He gave her a quick grin. Lissa must have spread the word, just like he'd thought she would. "Word gets around."

Celine rolled her eyes.

The door opened and his mother held out her arms. Jayson couldn't help a broad grin as Molly McBride hugged Celine first.

Celine seemed taken aback, but she recovered and hugged his mom in return.

"Mom." He grinned when the pair drew apart. "Apparently, there's no need to introduce my fiancée."

"Of course not." His mom took Celine's hands. "She's family now."

Celine looked speechless for a moment, then said, "It's great to meet you."

"It's Molly or Mom." She still held Celine's hands and studied her eyes. "I think you should definitely call me Mom," she said as if seeing that Celine needed some mothering, needed someone to call Mom.

Celine's throat worked as if she was choked up. She managed

a smile. "Thanks, Mom." She said it slowly, as if sounding out the word and seeing if it fit. Her smile softened as if it fit perfectly.

Typical of his mother, she swept Celine into the massive front room filled to the brim with his dad, brothers, sister, and few cousins, including Mike and his wife, Anna, as well as Creed and Danica. Not to mention kids, toddlers, and even an infant.

CELINE SAT on a couch with a group of young women who chatted and laughed and included her in their conversation, making her feel at home. She hadn't said a lot, feeling strangely shy, yet they'd made her feel a part of this different environment.

She had never been around so many down-to-earth, friendly, genuine people in all her life.

Her social world had been filled mostly with superficial women and arrogant men. She had one close friend, and that was it. Lots of acquaintances surrounded her in her life, but that's all they were—acquaintances.

So far, she'd met all of Jayson's brothers, his sister, and his cousin Mike's wife, Anna, who was pregnant. And she adored them all.

These people were *real*. You got what you saw, and she liked what she saw a lot.

Yesterday, Celine had called her own parents to give them the news. Her mother and father had been even more distant than usual, if that was possible, when she told them she was marrying an Arizona rancher. Their reception of her news had been just as cold as she'd expected. She could practically hear their thoughts —that she was marrying someone *common*, someone probably after her money and her inheritance. She wouldn't be surprised if she heard from their lawyer that they were disowning her and cutting her off.

It would be just like them to send someone to do their dirty work. But it didn't matter. She planned to donate it all if it did end up in her hands.

She sighed to herself and pushed thoughts of her parents away. She had a new family, and she was bursting to the seams with such a strong sense of belonging with these wonderful people.

Mom and Dad. It sounded so good and filled her chest with warmth.

"Why don't you hold Emmy?" Bailey, who was holding a baby, a *baby*, stood next to Celine, catching her off guard. "She's Danica's youngest, and such a sweet little girl." She nodded toward the kitchen. "Danica is finishing up putting roses on a cake. She's incredibly talented."

Celine felt as if she'd just been asked to hold hot coals. "I—"

"Emmy is absolutely adorable." Bailey smiled, leaned down, and handed Emmy to Celine.

She had no choice but to take the infant. She held Emmy in her stiff arms, feeling like she was holding glass.

"Are you okay?" Bailey looked concerned as she knelt beside Celine's chair. She kept her voice low.

"I've never held a baby before." Celine swallowed. She felt incompetent and unworthy. "I don't know what to do."

Bailey didn't blink. "Oh, that's easy enough." She proceeded to demonstrate how to hold the infant. She put a cloth over Celine's shoulder in case Emmy burped up milk from her bottle.

Celine held Emmy against her shoulder like Bailey had shown her. She felt like a robot as she stiffly patted the baby's back.

"Relax," Bailey smiled as she stood in front of Celine. "You're doing great."

Celine let go of her breath and forced herself to release some of the tension in her body. She focused on the baby girl, who sucked on her knuckles and looked over Celine's shoulder.

"She's so tiny." Celine turned her head just enough to breathe in Emmy's scent. "She smells like baby powder and ginger snaps."

Bailey laughed and Celine brought her attention back to the young woman. "Most babies smell like that to me, too." She tipped her head to the side. "Have you been around kids much?"

Celine shook her head and dove in with the admission. "I've never been around children."

"Well, you have no choice now. You're part of the McBride clan." Nothing seemed to phase or surprise Bailey. She looked around the room and swept her hand out in a motion that seemed to encompass all the kids. "There are a lot of the little monsters—I mean darlings—around at McBride family gatherings."

Celine couldn't help a laugh, then realized she'd relaxed. And that the baby had burped up formula. "Good call on the cloth," Celine said to Bailey.

"Just wait 'til one of the little monsters projectile vomits around you or on you." Bailey grinned. "The baby is usually just burping up formula, but wow—you have to see it."

Celine's eyes widened. "Projectile vomiting?"

Bailey nodded. "It's like the exorcist takes over the baby for about ten seconds." She held out her arms. "Danica just came out of the kitchen. I'll take Emmy back to her mommy."

Instead of feeling relief, Celine didn't want to let the baby go. She wanted to hug her and hold her all night. But she let Bailey take her from her arms, along with the spit-up rag.

Bailey held the baby so naturally, and bounced Emmy. "How many children do you and Jayson want?"

It was like they say—she felt like a deer in the headlights. She froze. "We haven't talked about it."

"There's time enough for that," Bailey said. "I'll get Emmy back to Danica."

Celine watched Bailey head off with Emmy. This was a whole new experience for her. She almost felt like she'd landed on another world.

*Bailey's words came back to her.* "How many children do you and Jayson want?"

Celine hadn't even thought about having children. Jayson hadn't brought up the subject and she had been too giddy over knowing that he would be her husband.

Did she want children? She was certain he did, and that early on he had mentioned kids. But it had been long before she ever thought the two of them would end up being engaged.

Celine watched the kids running around. A couple of toddlers played with blocks in a corner as three young boys and two girls were ushered outside by teenagers who said they'd be on a soccer team with the kids.

"How are you doing, sweetheart?" Molly showed up and Celine rose from the couch.

Celine smiled. "I'm enjoying meeting and talking to everyone in the family." She had made herself say "Mom" earlier to get used to it. And because she liked it a lot. Even Jayson's father had told her to call him Dad.

From the moment she'd met Molly, she felt like she'd come home

"Wonderful." Molly rested her hand on Celine's forearm. "Why don't you join us in the kitchen?"

Celine nodded. "I'd love to."


THE SUN WAS SETTING by the time Jayson and Celine said goodbye to the family members still at the McBride ranch. Jayson opened the passenger door for her.

"Wow." Celine sat back in the seat when Jayson climbed in. "Just wow."

Jayson looked at her, his lips tipping into a smile. "I'm taking that as a good 'wow'?"

She nodded. "I *love* your family, Jayson."

"*Our* family," he said. "This is our family now."

Celine smiled and relaxed. "It's good to be an almost-McBride."

Jayson laughed and guided the truck away from the ranch and home.

CELINE FIDGETED with her handbag as they followed the maître 'd into the exclusive Manhattan hotel's restaurant. "This is a mistake," she said to Jayson beneath her breath.

He touched the small of her back, causing warmth to spread through her. "I'm here, honey. You'll be fine."

"This is going to be a lot different than meeting your family." Celine spotted her parents from behind the headwaiter. "There they are." Just seeing their aristocratic-like faces took her back to the childhood feelings of being unwanted and just tolerated.

Charles Northland III stood to greet them when they arrived. His expression was actually welcoming, and he greeted Jayson warmly as he held out his hand. "It is a pleasure, Jayson."

*What is he up to?* Celine wondered and nearly narrowed her eyes.

Jayson took Charles' hand and gave him a firm handshake. Her father was never warm to anyone he considered beneath him. "Nice to meet you, Charles."

Celine leaned down and kissed Mother on the cheek.

"Darling." Helene Northland smiled at Celine and took her hand. "It is wonderful to see you."

*Okay, something is going on.*

Was an attorney going to pop out of a corner with a stack of papers showing that her parents were disowning her? She wouldn't be surprised.

"Hello, Mother." Celine said before politely disengaging her hand.

"Please do join us in a glass of this 2012 Jadot Louis Le

Montrachet Grand Cru." Charles gestured to the bottle of chardonnay chilling in a bucket of ice.

Celine almost shook her head in disbelief. For her parents to select one of the most expensive wines on the market to share with a "commoner" just about blew her mind. Charles pompous presentation of the wine, didn't surprise her.

She stood to the side of one of the two empty chairs at the table. The table sparkled with its finely-cut silver crystal and exquisite china.

Jayson helped her into her chair before taking his own. Charles had already seated himself.

As soon as Jayson's butt hit his seat, Charles said, "I did a little research, and I understand you run a multi-million-dollar operation in Arizona."

Celine's jaw almost dropped to the table, but she managed to keep her teeth clenched. She'd had no idea Jayson ran such a lucrative business. Frankly she hadn't cared one way or another. She cared about the *man* not his money. And her father had done research?

But this explained her parents' warm reception of her husband-to-be.

She gritted her teeth until her head ached from the pressure. They probably thought she'd considered him a "worthy" catch.

They were lucky she managed to maintain her cool. At least outwardly.

Celine had to take deep breaths to try and relax. The attempt didn't work. It was a wonder she didn't stand up and march out of the restaurant.

"I do all right." Jayson didn't say anything more.

"Don't be so modest." Charles paused for a moment for a waiter to pour wine in their glasses.

When the waiter retreated, Charles continued. "I take it the McBride family controls most of the Prescott valley."

Celine felt heat roll off Jayson, but he appeared to take it in stride. "I wouldn't say that." He switched the topic. "Your daughter is an amazing woman. Her success is impressive."

Helene had a shrug in her voice. "She has been playing with it for some time now. It is lovely she has a hobby she enjoys.

Heat crept up Celine's neck and she felt like her hair might burst into flames. She clenched her fists beneath the table hoping like crazy she wouldn't erupt in front of a restaurant full of people. Jayson placed his hand over hers, soothing her, calming her.

"It's more than a hobby, Helene." Jayson squeezed Celine's hand beneath the table. "Few have accomplished what she has. Not many fashion designers have their clothing line selected to sell in exclusive department stores."

Both Mother and Father turned their attention to Celine.

"Darling, you've never shared that information with us." Helene looked completely astonished. Dollar signs popped into her eyes. "Do tell."

Her father was likely working the math over in his head. "Which department store?"

"I'd rather keep it confidential." Celine gave a tight smile.

Helene sounded annoyed. "We're your parents."

"Exactly," Celine said.

Jayson jumped in. "Our wedding date is set for next summer."

"That's lovely." Helene's use of the word "lovely" had a condescending ring to it.

Dinner went downhill from there.

Later, Celine did feel it was important to let her father know about Monty and what he had done when he worked for Charles. She finished with, "He killed Sky."

Charles brushed that aside. "How *dare* he take from me." Her moneyed and privileged father was more concerned with Monty having stolen from them than for the horses Monty had killed, including the one so important to Celine's heart. "I must check to see if the statute of limitations has expired."

Jayson explained that Monty was in prison and would likely serve a considerable amount of time for the things he'd done.

"Not good enough," Charles ground out.

The evening continued to speed down that hill.

"Tell us about your future in-laws," Helen said at one point.

"Mom and Dad are wonderful," Celine didn't catch herself in time from referring to them like they were her parents, but whatever.

"Mom and Dad?" Helene said the words coldly, leaving a chill in the air.

"They have embraced me as one of their own." Celine sat straighter in her seat. "The McBrides are, to a one, great people."

"Of course, they are." Helene's expression was so rigid, it looked like her face might shatter.

And with that, the night hit rock-bottom.

Celine and Jayson politely declined dessert.

Jayson insisted on paying for dinner and left enough cash in the black check presenter to cover it. They said their good nights and left the restaurant.

Instead of returning to their room in the hotel, they took a walk around Times Square, Jayson holding her hand.

"I cannot believe them." The words exploded from Celine. "Or maybe I can. Their behavior was absolutely unacceptable."

Jayson squeezed her hand and smiled gently at her when she looked at him. "It's all right, Celine. You have a family in Arizona who embraces you for who you are. And you are one hell of a woman. I'm proud of you."

Celine let out a long breath and smiled in return. "You're right. And most importantly, I have you."

## CHAPTER 15

"*Bold and spectacular.*"
"*Innovative and fresh.*"
"*Beautifully interpreted.*"
"*Mouthwateringly sublime.*"
"*A distinct and thrilling voice.*"

The praise bounced around in Celine's mind like the champagne bubbles in her glass.

Jayson, dressed in the Armani tuxedo she had given him, placed his fingers on the base of her spine, keeping her grounded. He always looked fantastic in Wranglers and a T-shirt...but in an Armani tux? *Oh. My. God.* He had every single woman there turning her head. Even the old scions of the fashion world seemed to do a double-take.

The journey here had been beyond rocky, but when everything started to fall together, she knew it was going to be okay. After what had happened with Monty, her team had pressed forward even harder, everyone even more determined to make her line a success.

Celine had felt positive about the commercial shoot and thrilled with the preparation for the launch. After Monty was gone, everything had fallen into place like well-ordered dominoes.

However, the reception of this Celine Originals line by the world of fashion during this runway debut had blown her away. It almost was too much to take.

She smiled and nodded as many who made up an important part of the fashion world made a point of congratulating her and raving about what she'd done with her hand crafted traditional textiles combined with cutting-edge digital technology.

"Thank you," she said over and over, meaning it every time. She made appropriate small talk before the next person came up to her and raved about her line.

A few made catty remarks formed as praise, but Celine didn't let it bother her. She'd been around people like that all her life, and she knew it for what it was.

Overall, everything turned out beautifully, and things couldn't be any better. She looked up and smiled at her future husband, feeling a sense of being home. Wherever she was with this man, she was exactly where she belonged.

CELINE STOOD with her arms folded on the top railing of one of the corrals at the Arabaya boys ranch outside of Prescott. She'd realized her dream when she'd purchased the ranch using funds from the deal with the exclusive department store that now carried her line of clothing.

Her employees who ran the ranch made sure the teenagers didn't make the mistake Celine had. She didn't want any kid to experience that same heartbreak, or any horse to go through what Sky had.

She watched Darrell who practiced his showmanship astride a gray Arabian. She saw potential in the young man. A little work on his horsemanship, a lot more work on healing the troubles of his abusive past, and he would do well.

Abuse—his had been both emotional and verbal, something she knew something about. Many thought abuse had to be physical, but the other was equally bad. No child should be told they are worthless, or even that they are an inconvenience.

For her entire life, Celine had known nothing but wealth. She'd had everything a child could want—if her parents hadn't decided *she* was too good for *it*, but only because she was *their* child, wanted or no. She was too good for Barbies and Legos. Her parents insisted she must have handmade wooden or porcelain dolls that they made her keep on a shelf because they were too nice to play with, and much too expensive.

She'd grown up not knowing what "fun" was. She hadn't watched so much as a single TV show while she was growing up. Her parents thought she was above such common things that would hamper her education and threaten her intelligence.

*Dear God.*

Children of the royal family likely had less restrictions on what they were allowed to do or have than she'd had. Celine mentally shook her head. She wasn't sure if that analogy was a stretch. She'd watched Princess Kate dote on her children and what a proud mother she was. Celine envied that.

What would it have been like to feel a parent's genuine pride instead of being shuttered away as nothing more than an inconvenience? Knowing she had been just as unwanted as Darrell had been told he was?

Water under the bridge? Could she just let it go?

She didn't know. Maybe one day she would.

Now, as she watched the kids at the boys' ranch and the therapeutic Arabian horses, she thought about how different their lives and paths were and had been. They'd had tough beginnings while many might have considered hers easy.

She watched a boy ride a proud Arabian and thought about Sky, the multimillion-dollar Arabian she'd had while growing up.

When it came down to it, she and the boys were the same in

all that mattered. In love with horses that gave love only such a proud beast could.

Jayson settled his palm at her waist, drawing her attention to him. "You've done a good thing here, honey."

She turned to smile at him. "It doesn't feel like I've done enough, but it's a start."

"When you get out there and teach those kids like you plan to," he said, "you're going to enjoy that even more than watching."

She nodded. "Yes, I am." She shaded her eyes from the sun when she looked up at him. "Are you ready to go home? It's time for chores."

"My men will take care of it." Jayson squeezed her to him. "I have an idea."

"Oh?" She turned to face him and raised an eyebrow. "You're full of ideas."

"Let's take off." He took her hands in his. "We can pick anywhere in the world you want to go."

She smiled. "What's the occasion?"

"You." He pointed to her chest. "Me." He thumped his own. "We wanted to get married on the anniversary of the day we met, this summer. Let's forget waiting. Let's do it now."

Sunshine bright happiness flowed through her. "You know what I have to say?"

He grinned. He knew her too well.

She wrapped her arms around his neck and kissed him. "I'm ready when you are."

# EXCERPT: LOVED BY YOU

# CHAPTER 1

*Damn, she's gorgeous.*

Justice McBride watched, mesmerized, unable to tear his gaze from the dancer who commanded the small stage at the outdoor Christmas festival.

Who knew clogging could be so *hot*?

Her red hair shone beneath the Arizona winter sun while her short blue dress swayed and bounced around her firm thighs. Her feet moved at an amazing speed. The emcee had announced that the music she now danced to was *Lost Girls* by Lindsey Stirling. Good tune.

All Justice knew was that he couldn't look away.

*Rose.* The emcee had called her Rose.

The tap of her clogs as she moved around the stage spotlighted her abilities. He took in the sensuality of the woman in her every move, and studied her smile—mysterious and probably a whole lot of dangerous.

Yeah, there was a good chance she could tear out a man's heart as easily as pulling a brush through all that wavy red hair sliding around her shoulders.

Rose shot Justice a flirtatious smile as she danced by, blue-green eyes sparkling, before she spun away.

That one smile shot an electric sensation straight to his gut. *Damn,* she fascinated him. Her flirting had only been part of the show, but he had to meet her.

The energetic tune ended with an emphatic final tap of her shoes. The beautiful woman gave a slight bow to the crowd that applauded and cheered. The talented young dancer from a couple of previous numbers, who had equally bright red hair, ran up to Rose's side. The pair bowed together. Mother and daughter, clear as could be.

More cheers followed Rose as she exited, while the girl ran to the back of the stage. The emcee had earlier announced her to the crowd as Sophie.

Justice worked to get past observers in the crowd, hoping one of his many cousins or numerous friends wouldn't waylay him. He had to get to Rose before she left the area.

Hell if he knew why it was so important to him. He'd never felt this compelled to meet a woman. It was as if someone, something, pushed him forward.

A wooden box carved with Celtic designs sat in one corner. Sophie scooped up the box then walked it around the stage. Men and women of all ages threw coins and bills into the box.

Justice hurried to pull a twenty from his pocket and tossed it in. The girl's face lit with a spectacular smile. Yep, no doubt. She was related to the woman he had to meet.

He nodded to the girl and returned her smile before winding through the onlookers, most of whom were here for the Prescott Christmas Festival. Holiday cheer was in abundance with lots of laughter and good spirits.

Justice spotted Rose standing behind the stage's backdrop, her back to him as she kicked off her clogs then dropped them into a duffel bag. She slipped on some flats and shrugged into a black jacket.

She pushed her long hair away from her face and let it flow down her back. He imagined sliding his fingers through all that thick red hair and his gut tightened.

A man, who must have been in his early thirties, walked from behind the stage, as if waiting for Rose. He sauntered until he stood behind her. He paused, staring at her backside as she bent and picked up the duffel bag.

Justice scowled. The way the man stared at Rose was nothing short of lewd. It made Justice want to slam his fist into the man's jaw.

The man grinned, reached his hand under Rose's short skirt, and grabbed her ass.

Rose's back went ramrod straight and she dropped the bag.

Heat slammed into Justice. His scalp prickled. He didn't tolerate anyone treating a lady with anything less than respect. He ground his teeth as he started toward Rose and the man. *Sonofabitch.*

The redhead turned to face the man and smiled. It wasn't meant to be pleasant. It was a smile that would likely scare the shit out of most men. She shot out her hand, and in one smooth move she grabbed the man's index finger and drove him to his knees so fast that Justice stopped in his tracks.

The asshole let out a screech of pain.

"Touch me again," Rose said with an Irish accent, "and I will break your finger right before I make it quite impossible for you to ever father a child."

The man glared up at her. "Let go, bitch."

"I do believe you've got a death wish," she said before twisting his finger harder.

He cried out again before she released him. "Fuck you," he growled as he held his hand to his chest.

"Not on your life." Rose waved him away like a witch dismissing a demon spirit. "Begone."

Justice grinned as the idiot fled. Even then, Justice fought the urge to follow him and kick his ass.

The man tossed an angry look over his shoulder, and then he was gone, lost in the crowd around them.

*So much for the Christmas spirit.*

The young girl darted past Justice before he could reach Rose. Sophie carried the now closed wooden box as she ran to the woman's side. Rose's expression shifted from pissed to pleasant as she greeted the girl with a smile.

"Mama, I like this Prescott town." She looked up at her mother as she held up the box. "The people are very generous here."

"That's wonderful, Sophie." Rose's words now had a softer lilt to them as she handed the girl a jacket. "Get this on before you catch your death of it. Time for us both to go back to our booth and take care of business."

Sophie set the box down and tugged on her jacket. She had a sprinkling of freckles across her small nose, and delicate features. The girl would be as beautiful as her mother one day.

She glanced at Justice, who had stopped just feet away. The girl nodded in his direction. "That nice man put twenty in."

Rose turned her head and her gaze met Justice's. She looked at him for a few heartbeats before saying, "That was kind of you."

"You're both very gifted." Justice tried to come up with something that didn't sound lame. "I'm impressed with your talent."

"Thank you." The wariness in her gaze told him something concerned her. Maybe she thought he was some kind of stalker.

Shit. How the hell was he supposed to do more than get a "thank you" out of the woman if she was resistant to even a little conversation?

"Nice to meet you, ma'am." He touched the brim of his Stetson. "I'm Justice McBride." He reached out a hand. "I heard the emcee call you Rose."

"Mama's real name is Fiona—" Sophie started, then stopped

and clapped her hand over mouth when her mother shot her a look. Sophie winced like she knew she'd just blown it. She lowered her hand and mouthed, *Sorry,* to Fiona.

He held back a grin. Fiona suited her much better than Rose.

"Call me Rose." Fiona took his hand. Her expression was reluctant, but her grip was firm. "A pleasure, Mr. McBride."

He liked the sound of her voice, and the feel of her soft hand in his that warmed him through. He let her go the moment she moved to withdraw her hand, even though he would have liked to hold it just a little bit longer.

"Would you and your daughter like to have lunch?" Justice smiled. "On me."

"Yes!" Sophie bounced up and down on her toes, a lot like his teenage niece when she was squealing with excitement. Sophie then glanced at her mother. "Please Mama?"

Fiona shook her head and zipped the duffel bag.

Sophie looked crestfallen. "I'm hungry."

"You know we have sandwiches in the booth, including your favorite peanut butter and honey." Fiona met Justice's gaze again. "I do appreciate the offer, Mr. McBride."

He pushed up the brim of his hat with his finger. "Justice, please."

She slung the bag over her shoulder. "What kind of a name is Justice?"

He shrugged. "I'll tell you one day."

With a shake of her head, she said, "Who says there's going to be another day?"

Now he was getting somewhere—he had her talking. He winked at Sophie then flashed Fiona a grin. "Sophie does."

"Yes." Sophie nodded. "Absolutely."

Fiona raised an eyebrow. "You're using my daughter's fascination with you to sway me?"

"Sophie and I are already buds." Justice slipped his thumbs

into his belt loops and rocked back on his boot heels. "I'd like to get to know you, too."

Fiona had a spark of laughter and something else in her eyes, but she managed to keep her feelings from showing in her expression. "We have work to do and we best be going, Mr. McBride." She rested her hand on her daughter's shoulder. "Come, Sophie." She started walking while guiding the girl along with her.

Justice fell into step beside Fiona. "Are you sure you don't want lunch? The Grand Saloon on Whiskey Row isn't just a watering hole. It has fantastic sandwiches."

Rose ignored him but didn't chase him off. They worked their way through the Christmas festival crowd, the people wandering from booth to booth. Vendors sold everything from oil paintings and professional photographs, to Christmas crafts and ornaments, to handmade furniture and hand-thrown pottery, to saltwater taffy and holiday cookies.

It was hard to believe the year had gone by so quickly. Thanksgiving was less than a week away. Holiday decorations had gone up the day after Halloween and they were in abundance in downtown Prescott.

The Christmas spirit was alive and well here. Chatter and exclamations, smiles and laughter. Couples holding hands, children running through the crowds, a dad swinging his daughter up and onto his shoulder.

Justice breathed in smells from nearby vendors—of roasted almonds, hot chocolate, and the pumpkin spice lattes his sister liked. The chill in the air was enough to warrant a medium-weight jacket. Being farther north than the Phoenix metro area, it was cooler here, usually in the sixties in November. Not bad at all.

He glanced at Fiona, who was a good head shorter than he. At least she didn't seem bothered by his presence. Maybe slightly annoyed, but so far so good.

"You mentioned a booth," he said.

Fiona looked at him and rolled her eyes. "You are nothing, if not persistent."

She was fun. Justice grinned. "Persistent is my middle name."

Fiona shook her head. "Justice Persistent McBride. Suits you."

"You have no idea." Another plus. She'd remembered his last name.

They walked up to a booth with a front case containing silver bracelets, necklaces, pendants, pins, and rings, some inlaid with various stones of assorted shades.

At the back was a white tent with flaps. A nicely made hand-decorated sign with gold outlined green lettering said, *Readings today.* Hmmm. Readings? Fiona must be a fortune teller or card reader. Sophie seemed a little young to be telling fortunes, but he guessed one never knew without asking.

He looked at Sophie. "Is this your booth?"

She nodded. "Mama and I make the jewelry."

"Shush, girl. Don't encourage the man," Fiona said before she walked around the display. She'd said it in a tone that was more amused than anything else.

Things weren't looking so bad. She could have taken him down to the ground the same way she'd put that idiot in his place. She hadn't tried once to hurt him. That had to be a good sign.

Fiona set the duffel bag on the ground and gave the woman behind the case a warm smile. "Thank you, Gisela."

Gisela got to her feet, steadying herself with a cane. "You're welcome, lovey." The old woman had an English accent, as opposed to Fiona's Irish lilt. "You had quite a few customers. Sales were good."

"That's super awesome." Sophie's green eyes lit up. "Thanks, Auntie Gisela."

The older woman patted Sophie's hand. "I best be helping

Nigel now. He probably sold all the handmade soap at half the price." She sighed. "Again."

Gisela walked outside the booth.

Justice touched the brim of his hat. "Ma'am," he said as she approached.

"Good day, young man." She gave a single nod and continued into the pathway, shoppers parting ahead like the Red Sea as she leaned heavily on the cane as she made her way to the booth closest to Fiona and Sophie's.

"She's not really my aunt," Sophie volunteered. She had none of Fiona's accent. "But we see her at most of the shows and she helps me and Mama sometimes. We do things for her, too."

"*Sophie.*" Fiona looked exasperated. "What is with that tongue of yours today?" She shooed the girl in the direction of the tent. "Put the box away, then we'll have sandwiches.

When Sophie was in the tent, Fiona met Justice's gaze. "I guess you'll be on your way now."

Sophie ducked out of the tent, now carrying a cooler. She ran to stand beside her mother.

The corner of Justice's mouth quirked. "As a matter-of-fact, I was looking for just the right gifts for some of the women in my family. I stopped by the festival to pick out something for my mom, sister, niece, and new sister-in-law."

He smiled at Fiona's skeptical expression before looking at Sophie. "Why don't you show me what you have? Maybe you can give me a few suggestions."

"I have lots of ideas." Sophie set the cooler on the ground and happily scooted around and stood behind the display. "I can tell you about our jewelry first."

Sophie explained the meaning behind each stone they used to make the pieces, the designs they used, and the Celtic influence in their art.

They used strictly silver to work with as opposed to white

gold, which they found was generally out of the budget for most people attending events like this one.

"Do you travel to different cities and towns to sell your jewelry?" He hadn't thought about this just being a stop along the road for Fiona.

The fact she wasn't local didn't make him want to get to know Fiona any less. And her daughter was great.

Sophie nodded. "All over the west."

Fiona put her fingertips to her forehead, as if counting to ten.

"You have an Irish accent," Justice said to Fiona who had lowered her hand. "Were you born in Ireland?"

Fiona shrugged. "I am as American as you are."

He studied her. How much of what she had told him—what little she'd told him—was real? After all, she'd claimed her name was Rose. "Where did you pick up your accent?"

"You certainly ask a lot of questions." A shadow passed over Fiona's features. "Have you decided on anything? We do not want to keep you."

Justice smiled. "I like what I see and with Sophie's help, I'm sure I'll find something they will like."

"How old is your niece?" Sophie asked Justice, after talking about their jewelry.

Fifteen minutes later, involving laughter between himself and Sophie—and Fiona shaking her head—Justice finished purchasing four different necklaces. He figured each suited one of the women in his family. But then what did he know about women?

He looked at the tent behind the booth and returned his gaze to Fiona. "You give readings?"

"Why?" Her expression shifted to both skeptical and amused. "I'm sure a cowboy like yourself doesn't venture into the metaphysical world."

"I don't know anything about it." He shrugged. "Doesn't mean I'm not open to learning."

Sophie moved beside Fiona and piped up, "It's twenty for a reading."

Fiona gave Sophie a *look*. "We've kept Mr. McBride far too long."

"I just happen to have another twenty." Justice pulled his wallet from his back pocket, drew out a crisp bill, and handed it to Sophie.

He gave Fiona a quick grin. "Ready to read me?"

# CHAPTER 2

Fiona studied the cowboy who looked at her with such genuine interest. And he'd hit it off with Sophie. The reading she'd done for herself early this morning flashed through her mind, and the man the cards had mentioned.

This cowboy couldn't be the king in the cards. Even if he was, she needed to send him packing. So, why hadn't she?

He adjusted the brim of his hat and she let him hold her gaze with his. Eyes, a deep shade of brown, so intense and striking, as if they were made of brown silk.

A leather bomber jacket hid his upper body or she might be even more unnerved. She'd checked out his ass more than once while Sophie had been showing him jewelry pieces. She could almost feel the tough denim beneath her fingertips as if she now caressed the material that lovingly clad his muscular thighs and hugged his tight ass.

*For goodness sake, Fiona, she told herself, you don't need to be noticing the man's ass.*

She had felt so much strength in his large calloused hand. She could imagine the rest of him being just as strong and hard.

Fiona mentally groaned.

She had only been with one man and that had been before she fled. There hadn't been time or opportunity since for a relationship, much less the desire to have one.

*And that includes now.*

Fiona could sense no guile, no trickery in Justice…nothing but honesty and straightforwardness. Integrity even. All things she knew little about from men.

She'd excelled at reading people for the past decade and had yet to be taken in.

*Not since Gilroy.*

*Don't let this be the first time. It could be your last.*

The thought chilled her.

*You believed in a man before, Fiona. And you nearly died. You could have lost Sophie.*

She'd been barely eighteen then.

*Some things don't change.*

*I have.*

Justice McBride had only been around her a mere thirty minutes or so. Yet, she had enjoyed his company and his interaction with her daughter.

But no, she couldn't let her guard down.

*Not now, not ever.*

She wanted to tell Sophie to give Justice back his money, but it would confuse her daughter. Truth be told, they needed it.

A dark thought crept into the back of her mind and grew as the memory floated in her mind of Gilroy's last threat, the leather strap, and his last punch. He'd had her flat on her back, on the floor of their trailer, his fist coming down, down…

Then he'd slammed it into her face. She could almost feel the pain of his brutal attack and the darkness that had started to close in on her. She'd been pregnant and she didn't dare fight back or he might have hurt the baby.

*Remember you can't trust.*

The chill that had entered her system started to ice over her heart.

Her throat worked as she swallowed.

*Get this over with.*

Justice looked at her in a way that made her feel as if he could see every question, every bit of confusion in her mind, heart, and soul.

"Are you all right, Fiona?" His voice was softer, concerned.

His calmness and the use of her real name jarred her back to reality. It seemed like they had been standing still, staring at each other for at least an hour. But the thoughts swirling in her mind couldn't have taken more than a minute.

"It's Rose." Fiona straightened her spine. "Of course, I'm fine. Are you sure you want a reading, Mr. McBride?"

"Justice," he said once again. "I'm positive I'd like that."

"Give me a moment." She turned to go into the tent. She came up short when he stepped around and reached the tent before her. He pulled the flap back, then held it open. She hesitated, unused to what should have been a common courtesy.

*Common courtesies.* That was one subject she didn't know a lot about when it came to men.

"Thank you," she said. "I'll be right with you," she added before she ducked into the tent. Sounds of the Christmas festival were dampened here, enough that she could focus more easily when she had clients, or needed to meditate.

Fiona kicked off her flats and took a moment to strip out of the blue and gold dress she had danced in. She went to a carved wooden chest below the colorful sheers at the back of the tent, and put the clothes in one corner. Before she closed the lid, she pulled out a soft, billowy gown, slipped it over her head, then belted it with a tie of the same opaque purple material.

She picked up a set of gold bracelets that had been lying next to the pillar candle she'd anointed. She slipped the bangles on, and they clanged like little bells as they slid down her wrist.

Her tent was easy to set up and take down, but she had decorated it in a way that its energy called to her inner self. Every show, each time they set up, she hung colorful sheer silk scarves around the space and draped a purple silk cloth over the low round table at the center.

A short nearby shelf held both rose and clear quartz, as well as tiger-eye, tanzanite, and amethyst stones. The stones' vibrations and energy leant her strength and clarity. She lit a candle, drawing the scent of the citron oils as the flame grew.

When she was ready, she walked barefoot across the large soft purple rug on the tent floor and opened the flap. "You may come in now." Justice took his cowboy hat off as he entered, and she pointed to his boots. "You'll be more comfortable with them off."

He smiled and spoke in his low drawl. "If you say so."

Fiona managed not to give him a smile of her own. "I say so."

At the low table, she settled cross-legged onto her favorite seat, a comfortable Bohemian fabric pouf. She loved poufs, which were cushions, like shorter and softer ottomans. She grabbed her cards and shuffled them with quick efficiency.

Almost every day for the past eleven years, after she learned and started practicing the art, she had meditated on her own as well as giving readings. She'd been a natural at reading tarot cards. They spoke to her.

While Justice removed his boots, Fiona focused on the well-loved deck and held it in her left hand as she breathed in the scent of the magnolias. Usually, the peaceful smell relaxed her and allowed her to fall more easily into each reading she performed, including her own. She liked the flowers' scent, but it gave an entirely different vibe now.

She held her right hand over the deck, clearing it of any negative energy the previous client may have left. She mentally imagined the white light of energy traveling from her palm to the deck, and invited in the healing power of the angels while vanquishing any negativity.

Those who read the messages in the tarot cards usually identified with one card in particular. Fiona's was the High Priestess, the Mystic.

Justice had settled across from her, and set his hat on the floor beside him. He looked surprisingly at ease as he situated himself at the low table and crossed his legs before it. Everything about him radiated confidence, but not cockiness. He was self-assured, comfortable in his own skin, as if he didn't need to prove anything to anyone.

*Refreshing.*

Her ability to analyze, assess, and come to conclusions about the people she met had served her well over the past decade. Any mistakes she'd made had been long ago, when she was young and had thought she could trust her judgment.

Now she was cautious, confident in her abilities, but never let her guard down.

So, what was it with Justice McBride? She felt nothing but peace from him.

Her radar was never off. Never.

"I like this." He looked around the space, his gaze taking in everything around them. "It's you."

"It makes me happy." Fiona surprised herself with the admission. "The positive energy in here gives me clarity and strength."

"It feels comfortable." He nodded. "Like you."

"Thank you." Why did his comment cause warmth to flow over her?

Fiona gripped the tarot deck. "Why do you want a reading?"

"I've never had one," he said. "I like to try new things, and I have to admit, I'm curious." He sounded genuinely interested.

"All right." Why did her hands shake? "Let's answer your curiosity."

"I'm ready when you are," he said.

She was aware of Justice closely watching as she rested the deck of oversized cards in one open palm. She brought the deck close to her chest and ran her thumb over one corner, greeting each card.

She looked at Justice. Her throat felt dry and unused. She swallowed and was glad her words came out clearly. "I want you to ask or think a question."

He looked as if considering, then nodded. "Done."

Too bad he hadn't verbalized the question. She would have loved to hear him say it in his smooth voice with his sexy cowboy drawl. The cards would tell her anyway.

Fiona shuffled the deck, asking for help and guidance from the angels so that she might give him the answers he sought. She let light flow into her body, the cards' energy making her own stronger as they spoke to her. Words, feelings, thoughts slid into her mind, random yet with a fluid consistency. The cards told her to stop shuffling and to do a heart spread.

*A heart spread?* She halted. A love reading—either about a relationship he was in, or questions about a relationship he was interested in starting.

She mentally frowned to herself. She had no idea why she didn't want to do that pattern. Well, she did know, but she refused just the same.

Maybe she was being silly. There was a woman in his life and he had questions about that person. But if he did, why would he be showing interest in Fiona?

She decided to do a three-card spread.

*"If you insist,"* the cards seemed to say to her in her mind.

She fanned out the deck and held it out to Justice. "Pick three cards. Do not look at them."

He appeared thoughtful as he chose one at a time and handed them to her. Her bracelets jangled in the silence as she put the cards face down on the table.

*She really didn't want to do this. Breathe, Fiona. This man is not the king from your own reading.*

Her hand trembled slightly as she turned over the first card.

*The Lovers.*

She nearly groaned.

*The second. The King of Pentacles.*

*Please, no.*

*The third. The High Priestess.*

Fiona closed her eyes and breathed in slow and deep, wondering how she was going to deal with this. *The future is fluid,* she reminded herself. *Send him packing.*

She raised her eyelids and met Justice's gaze. She wanted desperately to make something up, but she always told the truth about the client's future. The cards never went so far as to tell her how the person's life might end, thank God. But the cards that did speak to her insisted on honesty.

*Honesty.*

Her throat worked as she swallowed down the fluttering sensation that rose from her chest. "A relationship is in your future." She braced her palms on her knees as she summarized rather than telling him his future in detail. "This is the Lovers card. You will meet someone soon, your soul mate."

"I already have," he said quietly.

"Good for you," she snapped, then forced her temper down. The anger came from nowhere. She felt out of control, like she was a puppet on a string, forced to dance to someone else's tune.

Justice waited for her to continue, his presence somehow calming.

"The future isn't set," she said as pleasantly as possible. "I can only tell you the potential outcome."

He nodded. "Go ahead."

She slid her finger over the next card. "The King of Pentacles represents you." It had also turned up in her own reading earlier this morning, and represented a successful, ambitious man.

Nope. She didn't need a man obsessed with money. She'd send him packing.

The cards chided her. The King of Pentacles appreciated the

sensual, luxurious side of life, too. She'd felt that the moment she'd looked at the card.

Finally, she rested her finger on the third card, the one she had always identified with. "The High Priestess is the woman you will meet. She will resist you. She will challenge you."

"I can see that." He spoke as if he *knew.* Well, maybe he thought he did. Some people were intuitive, but that didn't mean they were right, or that the situation wouldn't change from their perceived outcome.

"You'll be lucky if the woman gives you the time of day." Fiona shrugged. "That's all I can tell you."

He grinned. "You've told me enough."

"Good." She stood, feeling unsteady as she rose. He picked up his hat and eased to his feet, as well. "You'd best be on your way then," she said.

He said nothing as he pulled on his boots. When he was finished, he studied her. "Why don't you and Sophie have dinner with me tonight?"

"We're busy." She hurried to force the words out. "I need to help Sophie now, but I have something to do first."

"All right." He stood at the entrance to the tent. "I'll see you tomorrow."

Her stomach flipped. "Not likely."

He smiled then opened the flap and let in the chilly air. He winked before slipping out and letting the flap close behind him.

She felt like a piece of her had just walked away.

Fiona gripped the deck in one hand while she used her other to rub her temples. She started to put the cards away when one slipped out and fell to the tent floor.

*The tower.*

Her blood chilled as words slipped in and out of her thoughts. *Darkness, destruction, on a physical scale. A time of great turmoil... shaking the foundation of her current sense of safety.* She desperately reached for the positive aspects of the Tower, but the cards didn't offer anything reassuring when they spoke to her.

She struggled to determine if the Tower had anything to do with the king in her own reading. The cards gave her a definite *no.* They still told her to allow the King of Pentacles into her life. That he was good, he was the light.

Then what was the Tower card all about?

Her throat worked as she swallowed.

She picked up the card, slipped it into the deck, then shoved it into the velvet bag. She pulled the drawstring tight before setting the pouch on the shelf next to the candle.

Fiona closed her eyes as she pushed aside thoughts of the Tower and focused on Justice. Everything told her he was the man in her own reading.

No. She would not allow him into her life.

She could only think of one thing to do.

*Run.*

Read more of *Loved by You!*

## ALSO BY CHEYENNE MCCRAY

∼

*(in reading order)*

~Contemporary Cowboys~

**"King Creek Cowboys" Series**
**The McLeods**

*Country Heat*

*Country Thunder*

*Country Storm*

*Country Rain*

*Country Monsoon*

*Country Mist*

*Country Lightning*

*Country Frost (coming winter 2024)*

**"Riding Tall 2" Series**
**The McBrides Too**

*Amazed by You*

*Loved by You*

*Midnight With You*

*Wild for You*

*Sold on You*

**"Riding Tall" Series**

### The McBrides

*Branded For You*

*Roping Your Heart*

*Fencing You In*

*Tying You Down*

*Playing With You*

*Crazy For You*

*Hot For You*

*Made For You*

*Held By You*

*Belong To You*

### "Rough and Ready" Series
### The Camerons

*Silk and Spurs*

*Lace and Lassos*

*Champagne and Chaps*

*Satin and Saddles*

*Roses and Rodeo* (with Creed McBride from **"Riding Tall" Series**)

*Roses and Rodeo* (with Creed McBride)

*Lingerie and Lariats*

*Lipstick and Leather*

~Romantic Suspense~

### "Sworn to Protect Series"

*Exposed Target*

*Shadow Target* coming 2024

*Lethal Target* coming 2025

*Moving Target* coming 2025

### "Deadly Intent" Series

*Hidden Prey*

*No Mercy*

*Taking Fire*

*Point Blank*

*Chosen Prey*

### "Armed and Dangerous" Series

*Zack*

*Luke*

*Clay*

*Kade*

*Alex* (a novella)

*Eric* (a novella)

### "Recovery Enforcement Division" Series

*Ruthless*

*Fractured*

*Vendetta*

### Save by purchasing Boxed Sets

Riding Tall 2 Box Set Volume One

*Amazed by You*

*Loved by You*

*Midnight with You*

Riding Tall 2 Box Set Volume Two
*Wild for You*
*Sold on You*

Riding Tall the First Boxed Set
Includes
*Branded for You*
*Roping Your Heart*
*Fencing You In*

Riding Tall the Second Boxed Set
Includes
*Tying You Down*
*Playing with You*
*Crazy for You*

Riding Tall the Third Boxed Set
Includes
*Hot for You*
*Made for You*
*Held by You*
*Belong to You*

Rough and Ready Boxed Set One
Includes
*Silk and Spurs*
*Lace and Lassos*
*Champagne and Chaps*

Rough and Ready Boxed Set Two

Includes

*Satin and Saddles*

*Roses and Rodeo*

*Lingerie and Lariats*

Armed and Dangerous Box Set One

Includes

*Zack*

*Luke*

*Clay*

Armed and Dangerous Box Set Two

*Kade*

*Alex*

*Eric*

~Romantic Suspense~

Deadly Intent Box Set 1

*Hidden Prey*

*No Mercy*

*Taking Fire*

Deadly Intent Box Set 2

*Point Blank*

*Chosen Prey*

Recovery Enforcement Division: the Collection

*Ruthless*

*Fractured*

*Vendetta*

~Paranormal Romance~

**"Dark Sorcery" Series**

*The Forbidden*

*The Seduced*

*The Wicked*

*The Enchanted* (novella)

*The Shadows*

*The Dark*

*Cheyenne Writing as Debbie Ries*

∼

~Shawna Taylor Cozy Mysteries~

*Cooking up Murder*

*Recipe for Killing*

*Pinch of Peril*

*Delicious Death*

*Taste of Danger*

# ABOUT CHEYENNE

**Cheyenne McCray** is an award-winning, *New York Times* and *USA Today* best-selling author who grew up on a ranch in southeastern Arizona and has written over one hundred published novels and novellas. Chey also writes cozy mysteries as **Debbie Ries**. She enjoys creating stories of suspense, love, and redemption with characters and worlds her readers can get lost in.

Chey and her husband live with their two Ragdoll cats, two corgis, and two poodle-mixes in southeastern Arizona. She enjoys going on long walks, traveling around the world, and searching for her next adventure and new ideas, as well as building miniature houses, quilting, and listening to audiobooks.

Find out more about Chey, how to contact her, and her books at **https://cheyennemccray.com.**

*Sign up for Cheyenne's Newsletter
to keep up with Chey and her latest novels*
*http://cheyennemccray.com/newsletter*

Made in United States
Troutdale, OR
07/25/2024